Chills and Thrills

Ye Gho

Chills and Thrills

THE ULTIMATE ANTHOLOGY OF THE MYSTICAL, MAGICAL, EERIE, & UNCANNY

Edited by
LENA TABORI &
NATASHA TABORI FRIED

Designed by
TIMOTHY SHANER

A WELCOME BOOK
NEW YORK

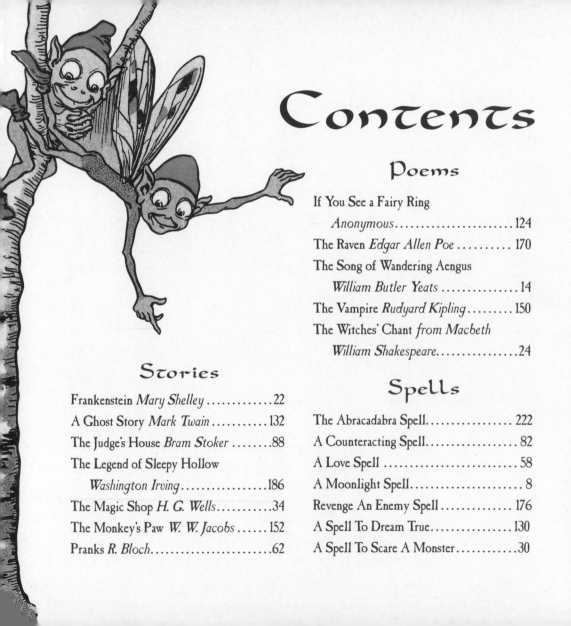

Contents

Poems

Stories

Spells

Magic Tricks

Curses

Treats

Superstitions

Legends & Lore

Introduction

Ghost stories, superstitions, tricks of illusion, and things that go bump in the night. They're a delicious part of every childhood. But while our love and fascination with mystery and magic may begin when we are young, it can last a lifetime. As a teenager I loved Tolkien and as an adult I was as much a Harry Potter addict as my fabulous teenage godchild, awaiting the release of each new volume with giddy anticipation. I don't think I will ever tire of the fantasy that there is a world beyond this one filled with fabulous beasts and mystical landscapes, where children can be wizards, dragons can be pets, and cars can fly through the sky like airplanes, not to mention talking paintings. It is in this spirit that we created *Chills and Thrills* with the best collection of scary stories, magic tricks, spells, superstitions, and legends we could find to enchant readers young and old (and aspiring wizards and witches!).

Real legends and curses, like those surrounding the discovery of King Tut's Tomb, are tucked between such terrifying classic tales as "The Monkey's Paw" and "Pranks." For the practicing sorcerer, we've included some useful basic charms and spells. "Revenge an Enemy," for instance, may come in handy in the schoolyard, while "A Spell to Dream True" is a bedtime requirement. Fans of Houdini will devour the simple magic tricks like making a friend float in mid-air or an egg fly. You'll adore the bewitched recipes: Graveyard Brownies that magically melt in your mouth, Roasted Pumpkin Seeds that make the perfect Halloween snack, delicious Eyeball Cookies, and many more. Finally, there are the stories behind common superstitions and even a few enchanted poems by such literary greats as Yeats, Shakespeare, and Kipling.

So turn down the lights, lock all the doors and prepare to be seriously spooked. This wondrous little book will terrify, delight, and entertain you and your family for years to come.

—LENA TABORI, publisher

A Moonlight Spell

Moonlight is
the special ingredient of
many spells and charms. For instance,
reflecting moonlight off a mirror onto the face of a
sleeping person will put that person under your spell.
Moonlight can also be captured in water and used in a variety of
magical recipes. Place a full jar of water outdoors beneath a full
moon and let it soak up the moonbeams all night. Then recite aloud,
"Moon spirits from up above, fill this jar with magic and love." Keep
the jar tightly sealed until you need it to perform a spell or create a
brew. One excellent mystical recipe that requires full moon water
is Psychic Tea. Heat one cup of full moon water with ¼ cup of
mint leaves and a sprinkle of sugar. Simmer for fifteen minutes and strain. Drinking this tea before performing
any psychic work will help focus the vision
of your inner eye and heighten
your senses.

THE CURSE OF
THE TOWER OF LONDON

The massive Tower of London is perhaps the most infamous and terrifying haunted dwelling in history. Built over a 200 year period that began in the early 11th century, this architectural wonder has 20 towers and occupies over 18 acres of land. Used by the English Monarch as a prison, the Tower of London has housed some of Britain's most notorious criminals. Murderers and traitors to the crown would find themselves hopelessly locked away in one of its many stone towers as they awaited their day of execution. Prisoners sentenced to death were beheaded within the Tower's formidable walls.

Many of those murdered on the block are said to haunt the Tower to this day. Lady Jane Grey, who held the throne for only nine days in 1554 before being executed in the Tower, is said to appear every year on the anniversary of her death, holding her head beneath her arm. Two other murdered queens,

Anne Boleyn and Katherine Howard, both wives of Henry VIII, also haunt the Tower as headless figures surrounded by a supernatural glow. Katherine has even been seen and heard wandering the halls begging for mercy as she did on the day of her execution.

One of the Tower's most gruesome murders was that of the Countess of Salisbury. As her head was placed on the block, the old woman panicked and tried to flee. The executioner chased her down and savagely hacked her to death with his bloody axe. It is said that spirits in the Tower still reenact her brutal killing for all to witness.

Of all the ghostly sightings in the Tower of London, the most disturbing is the apparition of two small boys walking along the hallways hand in hand. These children are widely believed to be the young sons of King Edward V. Edward's brother Richard, Duke of Gloucester, placed his young nephews in the Tower after King Edward's death. He later smothered the princes in their sleep, clearing the way for himself to assume the throne.

THE PHANTOM MESSAGE

Make words appear out of thin air in this trick that will give your audience goosebumps.

Before you perform the trick, prepare the magical note: Pour some lemon juice in a bowl and use it as "ink." Dip a toothpick into the juice and write on a piece of white paper. Keep the message spooky, such as:

I AM HERE. I CAN SEE YOU BUT YOU WILL NEVER SEE ME.

In front of your audience, announce that you are holding a message from the beyond. Push down the handle on your toaster, and hold the paper over the warm air above it.

The writing will magically appear.

The Song of Wandering Aengus
by William Butler Yeats

I went out to the hazel wood,
Because a fire was in my head,
And cut and peeled a hazel wand,
And hooked a berry to a thread,
And when white moths were on the wing,
And moth-like stars were flickering out,
I dropped the berry in a stream
And caught a little silver trout.

When I had laid it on the floor
I went to blow the fire a-flame,
But something rustled on the floor,

And someone called me by my name;
It had become a glimmering girl
With apple blossoms in her hair
Who called me by my name and ran
And faded through the brightening air.

Though I am old with wandering
Through hollow lands and hilly lands,
I will find out where she has gone,
And kiss her lips and take her hands;
And walk among long dappled grass,
And pluck till time and times are done,
The silver apples of the moon,
The golden apples of the sun.

BROOMS

With all the superstitions surrounding brooms, it's a wonder any housework gets done at all. You should avoid placing a broom against your bed because the broom's evil spirit will cast a spell on it. Don't let a broom sweep over your feet if you ever wish to be married, and never step over the handle of a broom lying on the floor because it's believed to bring death.

If you drop a broom, company will arrive. If you sweep trash out your door at night, it summons the visit of a stranger. And if you forget to sweep out the room where an unwelcome guest has stayed, that guest may return. To prevent additional bad luck, never take your old broom with you when you move. Purchase a new one, or avoid trouble all together and just use a vacuum cleaner!

GRAVEYARD BROWNIES

These magical treats will actually melt in your mouth!

12 Vienna Finger cookies (or other
similarly shaped oval cookies)
5 eggs
2 sticks unsalted butter, softened
8 ounces unsweetened chocolate
3 1/2 cups sugar
1 tablespoon pure vanilla extract
1 2/3 cups sifted all-purpose flour
1/2 teaspoon salt

1. Preheat oven to 400° F.
2. Grease a 9 x 13-inch pan.
3. Combine chocolate and butter in a double boiler and heat over simmering water until the mixture is completely melted. Remove from heat and set aside.
4. Beat eggs and sugar with an electric mixer at high speed for 10 minutes. Reduce to low speed and add the melted chocolate and vanilla. Blend well.
5. Add the flour and salt and mix until ingredients are combined.
6. Pour batter into greased pan and bake for 30-35 minutes or until edges are dry but the center is still soft.
7. Remove baking pan from oven and immediately press the Vienna Fingers into the brownies so that they are standing up like gravestones. Make sure you space the cookies evenly so that when you cut the brownies into squares, each piece will have one gravestone/cookie. Allow brownies to cool 20 minutes before cutting and serving. Serve with a large pitcher of milk.

Makes one dozen brownies

The Banshee

One of the most frightening and magical creatures in Irish and Scottish legend is the Banshee. Known as the fairy of death, a visit from the Banshee foretells the certain demise of a family member or loved one. Described as a beautiful young maiden in flowing white robes, the Banshee often delivers her death curse while floating above water or riding upon the back of a galloping steed. Only her crimson eyes betray her inhumanity, for otherwise she looks just like a normal woman. More horrifying than her appearance are the tortured wails and moans she cries out just before the moment of death. So the next time you hear a distant howl, think twice. It could be a neighborhood dog baying at the moon, or it just might be the Banshee coming to pay you a visit.

FRANKENSTEIN

BY MARY SHELLEY

It was on a dreary night of November that I beheld the accomplishment of my toils. With an anxiety that almost amounted to agony, I collected the instruments of life around me, that I might infuse a spark of being into the lifeless thing that lay at my feet. It was already one in the morning; the rain pattered dismally against the panes, and my candle was nearly burnt out, when, by the glimmer of the half-extinguished light, I saw the dull yellow eye of the creature open; it breathed hard, and a convulsive motion agitated it limbs.

How can I describe my emotions at this catastrophe, or how delineate the wretch whom with such infinite pains and care I had endeavoured to form? His limbs were in proportion, and I had selected his features as beautiful. Beautiful! Great God! His yellow skin scarcely covered the work of muscles and arteries beneath; his hair was of a lustrous black, and flowing; his teeth of pearly whiteness; but these luxuriances only formed a more horrid contrast with his watery eyes, that seemed almost of the same colour as the dun-white sockets in which they were set, his shrivelled complexion and straight black lips.

The different accidents of life are not so changeable as the feelings of human nature. I had worked hard for nearly two years, for the sole purpose of infusing life into an inanimate body. For this I had deprived myself of rest and health. I had desired it with an ardour that far exceeded moderation; but now that I had finished, the beauty of the dream vanished, and breathless horror and disgust filled my heart.

The Witches' Chant
Macbeth, Act IV, Scene I
by William Shakespeare

Thunder. Enter the three Witches.

FIRST WITCH
Thrice the brinded cat hath mewed.

SECOND WITCH
Thrice, and once the hedge-pig
whined.

THIRD WITCH
Harpier cries "'Tis time, 'tis time!"

FIRST WITCH
Round about the cauldron go;
In the poisoned entrails throw.
Toad, that under cold stone
Days and nights has thirty-one
Sweltered venom sleeping got,
Boil thou first i' th' charmèd pot.

The Witches circle the cauldron.

ALL
Double, double toil and trouble;
Fire burn, and cauldron bubble.

SECOND WITCH
Fillet of a fenny snake
In the cauldron boil and bake.
Eye of newt and toe of frog,
Wool of bat and tongue of dog,
Adder's fork and blindworm's sting,
Lizard's leg and howlet's wing,
For a charm of powerful trouble,
Like a hell-broth boil and bubble.

ALL
Double, double toil and trouble;
Fire burn, and cauldron bubble.

THIRD WITCH

Scale of dragon, tooth of wolf,
Witch's mummy, maw and gulf
Of the ravined salt-sea shark,
Root of hemlock digged i' th' dark,
Liver of blaspheming Jew,
Gall of goat and slips of yew
Slivered in the moon's eclipse,
Nose of Turk and Tartar's lips,
Finger of birth-strangled babe
Ditch-delivered by a drab,
Make the gruel thick and slab.
Add thereto a tiger's chaudron
For th' ingredience of our cauldron.

ALL

Double, double toil and trouble;
Fire burn, and cauldron bubble.

SECOND WITCH

Cool it with a baboon's blood.
Then the charm is firm and good.

Enter Hecate to the other three Witches.

HECATE

O, well done! I commend your pains,
And everyone shall share i' th' gains.
And now about the cauldron sing
Like elves and fairies in a ring,
Enchanting all that you put in.

SECOND WITCH

By the pricking of my thumbs,
Something wicked this way comes.
Open, locks,
Whoever knocks.

LADDERS

It is a widely known superstition that to walk under a ladder is bad luck. Historical explanations for this justify this sinister conclusion. To the ancient Egyptians, the shape of the pyramids was sacred, and to walk under a ladder would be to break the triangle it formed with the wall. This was an act they believed would have deadly consequences.

The Christians have a similar tenet, but believe it is the Holy Trinity (father, son, and holy ghost) that is violated when a ladder is crossed under. When you walk through the triangle, it is feared, you walk with the devil.

In more recent times, tall ladders were used to take the dead from the noose after they had been hanged. It was believed that if you walked under that ladder, the dead, swinging from the gallows above, would watch you pass, and then you, too, would meet your death. It was also feared that the body would fall onto those who crossed below.

THE CURSE OF
LADY TICHBORNE

In the year 1150, the saintly Lady Mabella Tichborne lay dying in her room at Tichborne Manor. For months she lacked the strength even to sit by her window and look out over her vast estate, an eden of rich farmland in Hampshire County, England. She summoned her husband, Sir Roger de Tichborne, and shared her dying wish: that a loaf of bread be given to all of the poor once a year on Lady Day, a feast day of the Virgin Mary.

Unlike his wife, greedy Sir Roger felt no compassion for the hungry and quickly schemed to put an end to her request. He told Lady Mabella that he would distribute an annual gift in her name equal to the amount of land she could walk upon holding a lighted torch. Assured that she couldn't get out of bed, the sly Sir Roger felt he'd heard the last of the matter.

But Lady Mabella shocked them all. She crawled out of bed, took the torch, and dragged her skin-and-bones body around 23 acres of the estate. To this day, this parcel of land is known as the Crawls.

Back in her bed, Lady Mabella gathered the household around her and uttered the Tichborne Curse. If the yearly dole of bread was ever stopped, the Tichborne family would die out.

So began the Tichborne Dole, an event that drew vagrants, gypsies, and other poor British inhabitants to Hampshire County every year on March 25th. The custom went on for 600 years, until the local government got fed up with the influx of riff-raff and shut it down in 1794. As a result, male Tichborne heirs began to die.

Edward Doughty, a Tichborne who had changed his name, realized the curse was in action when four of his brothers died without children. With the sudden death of his six-year-old son—the only remaining Tichborne heir—he reinstated the dole, which has been handed out ever since. Today, families from the neighborhood gather at Tichborne Manor on Lady Day with buckets, bags and pillowcases to collect a few pounds of flour sprinkled with holy water.

A Spell to
Scare Away
A Monster

Here's a handy spell to get rid of any monsters or boogey men who may be lurking under the bed or in the closet.

Before going to sleep, flick the bedroom light switch on and off thirteen times while reciting the following charm:

> Monsters lurking far and near,
> Your jaws of death I do not fear.
>
> There are no children sleeping here,
> So scamper off and disappear!

THE GHOSTLY MARK

This tricks makes a letter magically appear on the hand of someone in your audience.

Using a black magic marker, draw the letter "G" for Ghost on a sugar cube.

Secretly press your index finger on the G so that it leaves a mark.

Drop the sugar cube into a glass of water, saying "Melt, magical sugar, and make your sign appear somewhere in this room!"

Ask a friend to put his/her hand over the glass. Take the person's hand and press your index finger into her palm as you hold it.

Tell your friend to take her hand away and lift her palm. The ghost's signature "G" appears for everyone to see!

The Magic Shop
by H. G. Wells

I had seen the Magic Shop from afar several times; I had passed it once or twice, a shop window of alluring little objects, magic balls, magic hens, wonderful cones, ventriloquist dolls, the material of the basket trick, packs of cards that *looked* all right, and all that sort of thing, but never had I thought of going in until one day, almost without warning, Gip hauled me by my finger right up to the window, and so conducted himself that there was nothing for it but to take him in.

"If I was rich," said Gip, dabbling a finger at the Disappearing Egg, "I'd buy myself that. And that"—which was The Crying Baby, Very Human—"and that," which was a mystery, and called, so a neat card asserted, "Buy One and Astonish your Friends."

"Anything," said Gip, "will disappear under one of those cones. I have read about it in a book.

"And there, dadda, is the Vanishing Halfpenny—only they've put it this way up so's we can't see how it's done."

Gip, dear boy, inherits his mother's breeding, and he did not propose to enter the shop or worry in any way; only, you know, quite unconsciously he lugged my finger doorward, and he made his interest clear.

"That," he said, and pointed to the Magic Bottle.

"If you had that?" I said; at which promising inquiry he looked up with a sudden radiance.

"I could show it to Jessie," he said, thoughtful as ever of others.

"It's less than a hundred days to your birthday, Gibbles," I said, and laid my hand on the door-handle.

Gip made no answer, but his grip tightened on my finger, and so we came into the shop.

It was no common shop this; it was a magic shop, and all the prancing precedence Gip would have taken in the matter of mere toys was wanting. He left the burthen of the conversation to me.

It was a little, narrow shop, not very well lit, and the door-bell pinged again with a plaintive note as we closed it behind us. For a moment or so we were alone and could glance about us. There was a tiger in *papier-mâché* on the glass case that covered the low counter—a grave, kind-eyed tiger that waggled his head in a methodical manner; there were several crystal spheres, a china hand holding magic cards, a stock of magic fish-bowls in various sizes, and an immodest magic hat that shamelessly displayed its springs. On the floor were magic mirrors; one to draw you out long and thin, one to swell your head and vanish your legs, and one to make you short and fat like a draught; and while we were laughing at these the shopman, as I suppose, came in.

At any rate, there he was behind the counter—a curious, sallow, dark man, with one ear larger than the other and a chin like the toe-cap of a boot.

"What can we have the pleasure?" he said, spreading his long, magic fingers on the glass case; and so with a start we were aware of him.

"I want," I said, "to buy my little boy a few simple tricks."

"Legerdemain?" he asked. "Mechanical? Domestic?"

"Anything amusing?" said I.

"Um!" said the shopman, and scratched his head for a moment as if thinking. Then, quite distinctly, he drew from his head a glass ball. "Something is this way?" he said, and held it out.

The action was unexpected. I had seen the trick done at entertainments endless times before—it's part of the common stock of conjurers—but I had not expected it here. "That's good," I said, with a laugh.

"Isn't it?" said the shopman.

Gip stretched out his disengaged hand to take this object and found merely a blank palm.

"It's in your pocket," said the shopman, and there it was!

"How much will that be?" I asked.

"We make no charge for glass balls," said the shopman, politely. "We get them"—he picked one out of his elbow as he spoke—"free." He produced another from the back of his neck, and laid it beside its predecessor on the counter. Gip regarded his glass ball sagely, then directed a look of inquiry at the two on the counter, and finally brought his round-eyed scrutiny to the shopman, who smiled. "You

may have those too," said the shopman, "and if you don't mind, one from my mouth—*So!*"

Gip counselled me mutely for a moment, and then in a profound silence put away the four balls, resumed my reassuring finger, and nerved himself for the next event.

"We get all our smaller tricks in that way," the shopman remarked.

I laughed in the manner of one who subscribes to a jest. "Instead of going to the wholesale shop," I said. "Of course, it's cheaper."

"In a way," the shopman said. "Though we pay in the end. But not so heavily—as people suppose. . . . Our larger tricks and our daily provisions and all the other things we want, we get out of that hat. . . . And you know, sir, if you'll excuse my saying it, there isn't a wholesale shop, not for Genuine Magic goods, sir. I don't know if you noticed our inscription—the Genuine Magic shop." He drew a business-card from his cheek and handed it to me. "Genuine," he said, with his finger on the word, and added, "There is absolutely no deception, sir."

He seemed to be carrying out the joke pretty thoroughly, I thought.

He turned to Gip with a smile of remarkable affability. "You, you know, are the Right Sort of Boy."

I was surprised at his knowing that, because, in the interests of discipline, we keep it rather a secret even at home; but Gip received it in unflinching silence, keeping a steadfast eye on him.

"It's only the Right Sort of Boy gets through that doorway."

And as if by way of illustration, there came a rattling at the door, and a squeaking little voice could be faintly heard. "Nyar! I *warn* 'a go in there dadda, I WARN 'a go in there. Nya-a-a-ah!" and then the accents of a down-trodden parent urging consolations and propitiations. "It's locked, Edward," he said.

"But it isn't," said I.

"It is, sir," said the shopman, "always—for that sort of child," and as he spoke we had a glimpse of the other youngster, a small, white face, pallid from sweet-eating and over-sapid food, and distorted by evil passions, a ruthless little egotist, pawing at the enchanted pane. "It's no good, sir," said the shopman, as I moved, with my natural helpfulness, doorward, and presently the spoilt child was carried off howling.

"How do you manage that?" I said, breathing more freely.

"Magic!" said the shopman, with a careless wave of the hand, and behold! sparks of coloured fire flew out of his fingers and vanished into the shadows of the shop.

"You were saying," he said, addressing himself to Gip, "before you came in, that you would like one of our 'Buy One and Astonish your Friends' boxes?"

Gip, after a gallant effort, said "Yes."

"It's in your pocket."

And leaning over the counter—he really had an extraordinarily long body—this amazing person produced the article in the customary conjurer's manner. "Paper," he said, and took a sheet out of the empty hat with the springs: "string," and behold his mouth was a string-box, from which he drew an unending thread, which when he had tied his parcel he bit off—and, it seemed to me, swallowed the ball of string. And then he lit a candle at the nose of one of the ventriloquist's dummies, stuck one of his fingers (which had become sealing-wax red) into the flame, and so sealed the parcel. "Then there was the Disappearing Egg," he remarked, and produced one from within my coat-breast and packed it, and also The Crying Baby, Very Human. I handed each parcel to Gip as it was ready, and he clasped them to his chest.

He said very little, but his eyes were elo-quent; the clutch of his arms was eloquent. He was the playground of unspeakable emotions. These, you know, were *real* Magics.

Then, with a start, I discovered something moving about in my hat—something soft and jumpy. I whipped it off, and a ruffled pigeon—no doubt a confederate—dropped out and ran on the counter, and went, I fancy, into a cardboard box behind the *papier-mâché* tiger.

"Tut, tut!" said the shopman, dexterously relieving me of my headdress; "careless bird, and—as I live—nesting!"

He shook my hat, and shook out into his extended hand two or three eggs, a large marble, a watch, about half-a-dozen of the inevitable glass balls, and the crumpled, crinkled paper, more and more and more, talking all the time of the way in which people neglect to brush their hats *inside* as well as out, politely, of course, but with a certain personal application. "All sorts of things accumulate, sir. . . . Not *you*, of course, in particular. . . . Nearly every customer. . . . Astonishing what they carry about with them. . . ." The crumpled paper rose and billowed on the counter more and more and more, until he was nearly hidden from us, until he was altogether hidden, and still his voice went on and on. "We none of us know what the fair semblance of a human being may conceal, sir. Are we all then no better than brushed exteriors, whited sepulchres—"

His voice stopped—exactly like when you hit a neighbour's gramophone with a well-aimed brick, the same instant silence, and the rustle of the paper stopped, and everything was still. . . .

"Have you done with my hat?" I said, after an interval.

There was no answer.

I stared at Gip, and Gip stared at me, and there were our distortions in the magic mirrors, looking very run, and grave, and quiet. . . .

"I think we'll go now," I said. "Will you tell me how much all this comes to? . . .

"I say," I said, on a rather louder note, "I want the bill; and my hat, please."

It might have been a sniff from behind the paper pile. . . .

"Let's look behind the counter, Gip," I said. "He's making fun of us."

I led Gip round the head-wagging tiger, and what do you think there was behind the counter? No one at all! Only my hat on the floor, and a common conjurer's lop-eared white rabbit lost in meditation, and looking as stupid and crumpled as only a conjurer's rabbit can do. I resumed my hat, and the rabbit lolloped a lollop or so out of my way.

"Dadda!" said Gip, in a guilty whisper.

"What is it, Gip?" said I.

"I *do* like this shop, dadda."

"So should I," I said to myself, "if the counter wouldn't suddenly extend itself to shut one off from the door." But I didn't call Gip's attention to that. "Pussy!" he said, with a hand out to the rabbit as it came lolloping past us; "Pussy, do Gip a magic!" and his eyes followed it as it squeezed through a door I had certainly not remarked a moment before. Then this door opened wider, and the man with one ear larger than the other appeared again. He was smiling still, but his eye met mine with something between amusement and defiance. "You'd like to see our showroom, sir," he said, with an innocent suavity. Gip tugged my finger forward. I glanced at the counter and met the shopman's eye again. I was beginning to think the magic just a little too genuine. "We haven't very much time," I said. But somehow we were inside the showroom before I could finish that.

"All goods of the same quality," said the shopman, rubbing his flexible hands together, "and that is the Best. Nothing in the place that isn't genuine Magic, and warranted thoroughly rum. Excuse me, sir!"

I felt him pull at something that clung to my coat-sleeve, and then I saw he held a little, wriggling red demon by the tail—the little creature bit and fought and tried to get at his hand—and in a moment he tossed it carelessly behind a counter. No doubt the thing was only an image of twisted indiarubber, but for the moment—! And his gesture was exactly that of a man who handles some petty biting bit of vermin. I glanced at Gip, but Gip was looking at a magic rocking horse. I was glad he hadn't seen the thing. "I say," I said, in an undertone, and indicating Gip and the red demon with my eyes, "you haven't many things like *that* about, have you?"

"None of ours! Probably brought it with you," said the shopman—also in an undertone, and with a more dazzling smile than ever. "Astonishing what people *will* carry about with them unawares!" And then to Gip, "Do you see anything you fancy here?"

There were many things that Gip fancied there.

He turned to this astonishing tradesman with mingled confidence and respect. "Is that a Magic Sword?" he said.

"A Magic Toy Sword. It neither bends, breaks, nor cuts the fingers. It renders the bearer invincible in battle against anyone under eighteen. Half-a-crown to seven and sixpence, according to size. These panoplies on cards are for juvenile knights-errant and very useful—

shield of safety, sandals of swiftness, helmet of invisibility."

"Oh, dadda!" gasped Gip.

I tried to find out what they cost, but the shopman did not heed me. He had got Gip now; he had got him away from my finger; he had embarked upon the exposition of all his confounded stock, and nothing was going to stop him. Presently I saw with a qualm of distrust and something very like jealousy that Gip had hold of this person's finger as usually he has hold of mine. No doubt the fellow was interesting, I thought, and had an interestingly faked lot of stuff, really *good* faked stuff, still—

I wandered after them, saying very little, but keeping an eye on this prestidigital fellow. After all, Gip was enjoying it. And no doubt when the time came to go we should be able to go quite easily.

It was a long, rambling place, that showroom, a gallery broken up by stands and stalls and pillars, with archways leading off to other departments, in which the queerest-looking assistants loafed and stared at one, and with perplexing mirrors and curtains. So perplexing, indeed, were these that I was presently unable to make out the door by which we had come.

The shopman showed Gip magic trains that ran without steam or clockwork, just as you set the signals, and then some very, very valuable boxes of soldiers that all came alive directly you took off the lid and said—I myself haven't a very quick ear and it was a tongue-twisting sound, but Gip—he has his mother's ear—got it in no time. "Bravo!" said

45

the shopman, putting the men back into the box unceremoniously and handing it to Gip. "Now," said the shopman, and in a moment Gip had made them all alive again.

"You'll take that box?" asked the shopman.

"We'll take that box," said I, "unless you charge its full value. In which case it would need a Trust Magnate—"

"Dear heart! *No!*" and the shopman swept the little men back again, shut the lid, waved the box in the air, and there it was, in brown paper, tied up and—*with Gip's full name and address on the paper!*

The shopman laughed at my amazement.

"This is the genuine magic," he said. "The real thing."

"It's almost too genuine for my taste," I said again.

After that he fell to showing Gip tricks, odd tricks, and still odder the way they were done. He explained them, he turned them inside out, and there was the dear little chap nodding his busy bit of a head in the sagest manner.

I did not attend as well as I might. "Hey, presto!" said the Magic Shopman, and then would come the clear, small "Hey, presto!" of the boy. But I was distracted by other things. It was being borne in upon me just how tremendously rum this place was; it was, so to speak, inundated by a sense of rumness. There was something vaguely rum about the fixtures even, about the ceiling, about the floor, about the casually distributed chairs. I had a queer feeling that whenever I wasn't looking at them straight they went askew, and moved about, and played a noiseless puss-in-the-corner behind my back. And the cornice had a serpentine design with masks—masks altogether too expressive for proper plaster.

Then abruptly my attention was caught by one of the odd-looking assistants. He was some way off and evidently unaware of my presence—I saw a sort of three-quarter length of him over a pile of toys and through an arch—and, you know, he was leaning against a pillar in an idle sort of way doing the most horrid things with his features! The particularly horrid thing he did was with his nose. He did it just as though he was idle and wanted to amuse himself. First of all it was a short, blobby nose, and then suddenly he shot it out like a telescope, and then out it flew and became thinner and thinner until it was like a long, red, flexible whip. Like a thing in a nightmare it was! He flourished it about and flung it forth as a fly-fisher flings his line.

My instant thought was that Gip mustn't see him. I turned about, and there was Gip quite preoccupied with the shopman, and thinking no evil. They were whispering together and looking at me. Gip was standing on a stool, and the shopman was holding a sort of big drum in his hand.

"Hide and seek, dadda!" cried Gip. "You're He!"

And before I could do anything to prevent it, the shopman had clapped the big drum over him.

I saw what was up directly. "Take that off," I cried, "this instant! You'll frighten the boy. Take it off!"

The shopman with the unequal ears did so without a word, and held the big cylinder towards me to show its emptiness. And the stool was vacant! In that instant my boy had utterly disappeared! . . .

You know, perhaps, that sinister something that comes like a hand out of the unseen and grips your heart about. You know it takes your common self away and leaves you tense and deliberate, neither slow nor hasty, neither angry nor afraid. So it was with me.

I came up to this grinning shopman and kicked his stool aside.

"Stop this folly!" I said. "Where is my boy?"

"You see," he said, still displaying the drum's interior, "there is no deception—"

I put out my hand to grip him, and he eluded me by a dexterous movement. I snatched again, and he turned from me and pushed open a door to escape. "Stop!" I said, and he laughed, receding. I leapt after him—into utter darkness.

Thud!

"Lor' bless my 'eart! I didn't see you coming, sir!"

I was in Regent Street, and I had collided with a decent-looking working man; and a yard away, perhaps, and looking extremely perplexed with himself, was Gip. There was some sort of apology, and then

Gip had turned and come to me with a bright little smile, as though for a moment he had missed me.

And he was carrying four parcels in his arm!

He secured immediate possession of my finger.

For the second I was rather at a loss. I stared round to see the door of the magic shop, and, behold, it was not there! There was no door, no shop, nothing, only the common pilaster between the shop where they sell pictures and the window with the chicks! ...

I did the only thing possible in that mental tumult; I walked straight to the kerbstone and held up my umbrella for a cab.

"'Ansoms," said Gip, in a note of culminating exultation.

I helped him in, recalled my address with an effort, and got in also. Something unusual proclaimed itself in my tail-coat pocket, and I felt and discovered a glass ball. With a petulant expression I flung it into the street.

Gip said nothing.

For a space neither of us spoke.

"Dadda!" said Gip, at last, "that *was* a proper shop!"

I came round with that to the problem of just how the whole thing had seemed to him. He looked completely undamaged—so far, good; he was neither scared nor unhinged, he was simply tremendously satisfied with the afternoon's entertainment, and there in his arms were the four parcels.

Confound it! what could be in them?

"Um!" I said. "Little boys can't go to shops like that every day."

He received this with his usual stoicism, and for a moment I was sorry I was his father and not his mother, and so couldn't suddenly there, *coram publico*, in our hansom, kiss him. After all, I thought, the thing wasn't so very bad.

But it was only when we opened the parcels that I really began to be reassured. Three of them contained boxes of soldiers, quite ordinary lead soldiers, but of so good a quality as to make Gip altogether forget that originally these parcels had been Magic Tricks of the only genuine sort, and the fourth contained a kitten, a little living white kitten, in excellent health and appetite and temper.

I saw this unpacking with a sort of provisional relief. I hung about in the nursery for quite an unconscionable time. . . .

That happened six months ago. And now I am beginning to believe it is all right. The kitten had only the magic natural to all kittens, and the soldiers seem as steady a company as any colonel could desire. And Gip—?

The intelligent parent will understand that I have to go cautiously with Gip.

But I went so far as this one day. I said, "How would you like your soldiers to come alive, Gip, and march about by themselves?"

"Mine do," said Gip. "I just have to say a word I know before I open the lid."

"Then they march about alone?"

"Oh, *quite*, dadda. I shouldn't like them if they didn't do that."

I displayed no unbecoming surprise, and since then I have taken occasion to drop in upon him once or twice, unannounced, when the soldiers were about, but so far I have never discovered them performing in anything like a magical manner. . . .

It's so difficult to tell.

There's also a question of finance. I have an incurable habit of paying bills. I have been up and down Regent Street several times, looking for that shop. I am inclined to think, indeed, that in that matter honour is satisfied, and that, since Gip's name and address are known to them, I may very well leave it to these people, whoever they may be, to send in their bill in their own time. ☾

Merlin

In early Celtic tales Merlin was a poet, a prophet, a magician and a sage. At times he was also a hermit—at other times a conjurer and wizard.

It is believed that the myth of Merlin originated in the character of a Northern Welshman named Myrddin-or the madman and prophet of Scottish legend, Lailoken. He is believed to have caused the Battle of Arderydd in the 570s by provoking the British chieftains. As supernatural punishment, he lost his mind and was seen wandering the forests of Celidon in the Scottish lowlands.

But it is the story of King Arthur that turned Merlin into a true legend. As the sorcerer and court wizard who was Arthur's most important advisor, Merlin dwelled in enchanted places and used magic to manipulate nature. His powers of wizardry embraced both darkness and light (unlike his half-sister Morgan le Fay, a fairy witch, used her magical powers only to do evil). Merlin could change into a stag or a boy or any other creature, depending on his surroundings. He could also change others and make them invisible.

According to lore, King Uther was in love with Lady Ingraine, wife of the Duke of Tintagel. When she refused his advances, he called on Merlin for help. Using his powers, Merlin transformed Uther so he appeared to Ingraine as her own husband, and later Arthur was born. In exchange, Merlin asked the king to let him educate Arthur. So began the long relationship between Merlin and Arthur. The wizard trained Arthur as a knight and helped him prove himself and ascend the throne by giving him the sword in the stone. It was also Merlin who warned Arthur that the copper-haired beauty Guinevere would bring about his doom.

Later, Merlin himself fell for Nimue, Lady of the Lake. He proclaimed his love for her, but she was frightened and resisted him. Merlin made a spell to bind her to his side. Fearing his strength, the lake spirit begged him to teach her the secrets of his magic. He reluctantly agreed and led her to a silvery cave, where she put a spell on him that he himself had taught her. Merlin fell into a deep sleep and was imprisoned in the cave for eternity.

THE FLOATING FRIEND

They've seen it on TV, but you can bring it to their very eyes.

You'll need two sticks that are tall enough to reach from the floor to the neck of your magic show assistant.

Put a pair of shoes on the end of the sticks. Your friend straddles a bench and leans back until his head is resting on the bench. He holds the sticks along his sides. You have covered him with a sheet so the shoes on the end of the sticks stick out on one side and his head on the other.

You wave your magic wand or use your arms to cast a magic spell, motioning him to rise.

Your partner slowly stands up, holding the sticks straight out the entire time. With the sheet covering him, it looks like his whole body is rising from the bench.

SPIDER CAKE

Simple and delicious. Make one large chocolate spider web or
little ones on the corners of the orange frosting!

Cake
2 large eggs
$^2/_3$ cup sugar
$^2/_3$ cup butter
2 teaspoons grated orange rind
$^3/_4$ cup sifted cake flour
$^3/_4$ teaspoons baking powder
$^1/_4$ teaspoon salt

1. Preheat oven to 325°F.
2. Grease one 8-inch layer cake pan and dust
   with fine, dry breadcrumbs.
3. Mix eggs and sugar until light and fluffy.
4. Cream butter with orange rind.
5. In a large bowl, combine flour, baking
   powder, and salt. Add egg and butter
   mixtures and blend well with flour mixture.

6. Spoon batter into pan and bake for about
   25-30 minutes, or until a toothpick inserted
   into the center comes out clean.
7. Cool cake in pan for 10 minutes. Remove
   from pan and cool completely before icing.

Frosting
1 cup confectioners' sugar
2 tablespoons concentrated orange juice
2 squares of milk or dark chocolate

1. Mix sugar and juice until smooth.
2. Spread over top and sides of cooled cake.
3. Put 2 squares of milk or dark chocolate
   into a microwave-safe ziplock bag and
   microwave until warm and melted. Cut a
   tiny piece off the corner of the bag (or
   make a tiny hole with a toothpick) and use
   to paint your spider web on the icing!

Makes 6-8 servings

A Love Spell

Here's a spell that will bring the object of your affection right to your front door.

When the first snowfall of winter comes, build two snowmen in your yard or a nearby park. Make one in your image and the other in the image of the one whose heart you hope to capture. Each snowman must wear something that belongs to the person they represent. Sweeten the spot where the heart of each snowman should be with a little sugar and make sure that they are touching. Then light a votive candle (but do not leave the candle unattended). Recite this charm:

> By this candle that I light
> Let my true love now take flight.
> Lead my love on a magical tour
> Ending outside my front door.

By the time the candle has completely burned out, your beloved will have knocked upon your door.

GUESTS

Why are guests so well received at certain houses? The hosts may not be as polite as you think. They could just be superstitious.

Hundreds of years ago, people lived more simply and traveled very little. Communities were fearful of the mysterious world that existed beyond the boundaries of their villages. Witches and ominous gods were thought to live among the surrounding mountains, valleys, and seas. So when a stranger knocked on a family's door, people believed it could be a spirit coming to cast an evil spell on the home. Wanderers were therefore greeted as welcomed guests, and obliged with food and comfort in the hopes they would move on, peaceful and satisfied.

PRANKS

BY ROBERT BLOCH

The lights came on just after sunset.

He stood in the hallway, near the front door, filling the candy dish on the table with a skill born of long practice. How many times had he done this, how many Halloweens had he spent preparing for the joyful hours of the evening ahead? No use trying to remember; he'd lost count. Not that it mattered, really. What mattered was the occasion itself, the few hours of magic and make-believe one was privileged to share with the children. What mattered was the opportunity, however brief, to enter into the spirit of things, participate in the let's-pretend on the one night of the year when a childless couple could themselves pretend that they were truly no different from the members of the community around them; solid, ordinary citizens who took pride in their homes and their offspring.

But truth to tell, it was the make-believe that thrilled him. Maybe they both had a childish streak of their own, dressing up to surprise the youngsters.

Now, hearing her footsteps on the stairs, his eyes brightened in eager anticipation. One year she'd come sailing down the steps in hoop-skirts as Scarlett O'Hara, another time she'd gotten herself up as a black-braided Pocahontas, once she'd worn the powdered wig of a Marie Antoinette. What would he see tonight—Cleopatra, the Empress Josephine, Joan of Arc?

Leave it to her to fathom his expectations and astonish him with the unexpected. And that, as she descended into full view, was exactly what she did. For instead of a figure out of film or fiction he beheld a little old lady with a motherly smile, wearing an apron over a simple housedress, as though she had just stepped out of an old-fashioned country kitchen.

"How do you like it?" she said.

For a moment he stared at her, completely taken aback, yet puzzled by the odd familiarity of her appearance. Where had he seen this smiling elderly woman before? Then, suddenly, his gaze darted toward the candy dish on the table and the empty box beside it. And there on the front of the box was his answer—the oval photographic portrait purporting to represent the candy-maker herself. Tonight she was Mrs. See.

Now it was his turn to smile. "Marvelous!" he said. "It's hard for me to imagine you as an old lady, but I must say you look the part."

She nodded, pleased with his reaction. "I

think the kids will like it. And they certainly should be able to recognize you too, Ben."

He peered at her through the tiny rimless spectacles and patted his paunch. "I hope so. At least I make a better Ben Franklin than last year's Abraham Lincoln. Though I admit I was tempted to try something different for a change. Remember when I did Adolf Hitler—"

"And scared half the children out of their wits?" She shook her head. "Halloween's for fun, not fright. No, I think you made a good choice."

Then the doorbell rang.

She opened the door and the two of them stood side by side, gazing down at the little ragamuffin in the cowboy outfit as he clutched his crumpled shopping bag and rattled off the time-honored greeting. "Trick-or-treat," he said.

She stepped back, smiling. "Isn't he adorable?" she murmured. Then, "Come right in and help yourself. The candy's on the table."

The moment the front door closed, Joe Stuttman turned to Maggie, scowling. "Jesus H. Christ!" he said.

"Now, Joe, please!" Maggie sighed. "Don't get yourself upset over nothing."

"You call that nothing?" His scowl and

voice deepened. "Those damned costumes must have cost a fortune. I'm not blind, you know—I read the ads. Okay, so most of Angela's witch outfit you made yourself, but why in hell you had to go and buy Robbie that fancy space suit—"

"Simmer down," Maggie told him. "You don't have to pay for it. I've been saving up from my household allowance these past two months."

"So that's it!" Joe shook his head. "No wonder we've been eating so many of those lousy casserole messes lately. I work my tail off down at the shop and all I get to eat is glob because your son has to dress up like a goddamn astronaut for Halloween!"

"*Our* son," Maggie said softly. "Robbie's a good boy. You saw his last report card—all those A's mean he's really been doing his home-work. And he still finds time to help me around the house and do your yard work for you. I think he deserves a treat once in a while."

"Treat." Joe went over to the coffee table in front of the television set, picked up the six-pack resting there, then yanked out a can of beer. "That's another thing I don't like—this trick-or-treat business. Running up and down the street at night, knocking on doors and asking for a handout. I don't care what kind of a fancy getup a kid's wearing. What's he's really doing is acting like some wino on Main Street, a bum mooching off strangers. You call that good behavior? It's nothing but blackmail if you ask me." He thumbed the beer can tab. "Trick-or-treat—it's a threat, isn't it? Pay up or else. What are you training Robbie for, to grow up and join the Mafia?"

"For heaven's sake," Maggie said, "You don't have to go on a roll about it. You know as well as I do that trick-or-treat is just a phrase. People expect kids to ask them for candy or cookies on Halloween, it's just a tradition, that's all. And if somebody doesn't come through with a treat I'm sure neither Robbie nor Angela is going to do anything about it. They'll just go on to another house." She glanced unhappily toward the front door. "I only wish you'd let me put out a few little goodies for the kids who come here."

"No way," Joe said. He took a gulp of beer. "I thought we had that all settled. I'm not wasting my money on a mess of junk food for a bunch of little bastards who dress up in stupid costumes and come banging on my front door."

"But, Joe—"

"You heard me." Joe scooped up the six-pack with his free hand. "Now let's get those lights turned off, quick, before anyone shows up. I'm gonna watch the game on the set in the bedroom, and I don't want any interruptions. That means don't answer the door, do you read me?"

"Yes," Maggie said. "I read you."

It seemed to take forever for the twins to get ready; Pam's devil costume was too tight and had to be let out at the waist before it could be zipped up in back, and Debbie kept fussing with her clown makeup.

In point of fact, they didn't actually leave the house until almost eight-fifteen, but within three minutes after their departure Chuck and

Linda Cooper were in bed.

"Alone at last!" Linda giggled. "My God, you'd think I was some kind of floozy, sneaking around like this and waiting for a chance to hop into the sack the moment the coast is clear."

"Be a floozy," Chuck said. "Come on, I dare you."

"Don't get me wrong." Linda sobered. "You know how much I love the kids, we both do. But lately it seems like we never get a chance, what with their bedroom right next door to ours and these damned mattress springs squeaking. I'm always afraid they can hear us."

"So let them hear." Chuck grinned. "About time they learned the facts of life."

Linda shook her head. "But they're still so young! Maybe I'm too self-conscious, I don't know. It's the way I was brought up, I guess, and I can't help it."

"Look, let's not talk about it now, shall we?" Chuck tossed the covers aside. "I'm not going to spend the next two hours worrying whether or not the bedsprings squeak."

Sometime around nine-thirty Father Carmichael checked his watch. "Getting late," he said. "I really should be going. I thank you both for a lovely dinner and a delightful evening—"

"Come on, Father, what's your hurry?" Jim Higgins reached for the bottle and leaned forward to pour a good two inches of its contents into the priest's brandy snifter. "One for the road, okay?" he said.

Father Carmichael shrugged in mild protest, but Martha Higgins beamed and nodded at him from her chair beside the fireplace. "Please don't rush away, Billy and Pat should be home soon and I know they'd love to see you."

"I'd like that." The priest twirled his snifter, then raised it to drink, smiling as he did so. Then, as he set the glass down again, his expression changed. "Aren't they a little young to be out at this hour?"

"It's a trick-or-treat night, don't you remember?" Jim Higgins swallowed brandy in a single swig that emptied his own snifter. "After all, Halloween only comes once a year."

"Praise the Lord for that," Father Carmichael said softly.

Martha Higgins raised her eyebrows. "Don't you approve of trick-or-treat?"

"A harmless diversion," the priest told her. "But Halloween itself—"

"Now wait a minute." Jim Higgins spoke quickly, glancing at Martha out of the corner of his eye as he did so. "This is a nice friendly little town. You of all people should know that, Father. I realize a lot of parents go along with their youngsters on a night like this, but we talked it over and decided it was time for Billy and Pat to make the rounds alone if they wanted to. Sort of gives them a grown-up feeling, and helps them to understand there's nothing to be afraid of."

"Nothing to be afraid of." The priest sighed. Then, conscious of

Martha Higgins' sudden frown, he forced a smile. "Don't mind me," he said. "It's the brandy talking."

"What do you mean?" Jim Higgins was frowning too. "What's all this about Halloween? Are you trying to tell us we ought to be afraid of goblins and witches? I thought people stopped believing in that stuff a couple of hundred years ago."

"So they did." Father Carmichael took a hasty sip from his glass. "They stopped believing. But that in itself didn't necessarily stop the phenomena."

"But isn't a lot of that just superstition?" Martha said. "All this nonsense about vampires and werewolves and the dead coming out of their graves? And even if such things were possible, I don't see what it has to do with Halloween. It's just another holiday."

Father Carmichael finished his brandy before speaking. "The real holiday—holy day, that is—will come tomorrow, on the Feast of All Saints. It's then we celebrate Hallowmass in honor of Our Lady and all the martyrs unknown who died to preserve the faith. The faith which Satan abhors, because it affirms the power of Almighty God.

"But Satan too has power. And he chooses to manifest his defiance on the eve of Allhallows by loosing the forces of evil which he commands." The priest broke off, smiling self-consciously. "Forgive me—I didn't mean to start preaching a sermon. And I hope you realize I was just speaking figuratively, so to say."

"Sure thing," Jim Higgins moved to his wife and put his hand on her shoulder. "Just a little Halloween ghost story, right?"

Martha nodded but her eyes were troubled, intent on Father Carmichael as he glanced at his watch again, then rose.

"Time I was leaving," he said. "I take it I'll be seeing you both at Mass tomorrow—"

Martha gestured quickly. "But you haven't seen the children yet! They should be here any minute now. Please, Father. Won't you stay?"

The priest hesitated, conscious that the smile had faded from her face as he stared into the troubled eyes.

"Of course," he said. "Of course I'll stay."

Jim Higgins frowned. "Almost ten-thirty," he murmured. "They promised to be back by ten at the latest." The frown deepened. "You'll pardon my language, Father—but where in hell are those kids?"

"Heavenly," Irene Esterhazy said. "I mean heavenly." She lurched against the buffet table as she took another bite of her croissant. "Try one, honey—they're soooo good!"

Howard Esterhazy shook his head. "No time for that," he told her. "We've stayed too long as it is."

Once in the car, with the windows open and the night air fanning her face, Irene sobered slightly. "You mad at me, honey?"

"No." Howard sighed, eyes intent on the road. "I guess you're entitled to a little diversion once in a while. But do you realize what time it is?"

71

Irene focused her eyes on the illuminated dial of the dashboard clock. "My God, you're right! It's almost eleven. I had no idea—"

Her husband nodded, "I know. And I didn't want to spoil your fun. It's just that I told Connie we wouldn't be late."

"Maybe we ought to give her a little something extra," Irene said. "She always been so good about sitting with Mark, even though she does play that damn stereo full blast."

"You can say that again," Howard muttered as they pulled up before the house. The wind was rising, sending surges of sound through the treetops, but the screech of the stereo echoed so loudly that even their voices were drowned by its pounding beat as they left the car and moved up to the front door.

But as he fumbled in his pocket the door swung open quickly and Connie peered out, "Oh, it's you—" she said.

"I thought it was Mark." Connie's voice faltered.

"Mark?" Irene moved into the hall, her forehead furrowing. "You mean he isn't here?"

"Turn that thing off," Howard shouted.

Retreating to the living room, Connie hastily obeyed, then turned to confront the Esterhazys' accusing stare.

"Now what's all this about Mark?" Howard said. "Where is he?"

Connie's gaze dropped and her words came with forced bravado. "You know Bill Summers, that friend of his from down the street? Well, he came to the door and I thought it was trick-or-treat, but it turned out he wanted Mark to come out with him. Just around the block, he said, because he didn't want to go alone. I told Mark no, he wasn't supposed to, and he had all the candy he wanted right here at home that you left for him. Besides, he didn't even have a costume. But Bill said it would only be for a few minutes, and Mark was almost crying, he wanted to go so bad. So I figured why not let him just as long as he promised to come right back and not go off the block? Besides, I told my boyfriend where I was sitting tonight and he called on the phone right in the middle of all this going on, so—"

"Never mind that." Howard's hoarse voice held apprehension as well as anger. "How long ago was this?"

"How long?" Connie shook her head. "I don't know. I mean, I was on the phone and then I started playing the stereo, like maybe around ten o'clock."

"Then he's been gone over an hour." Howard's face was grim. "Maybe an hour and a half, while you sat there blabbing with your boyfriend and listening to that goddamn rock crap!"

Connie began to cry, but Irene ignored her. She turned to her husband. "Why don't you get in the car and take a run around the block? He can't have gone very far."

"I hope to God you're right." Howard moved toward the hall. "Meanwhile, you better phone the Summerses and see if Bill brought him back over there."

"Good idea. I never thought of that." Irene was already dialing as Howard started up the car outside, and she could hear it pulling away as Mrs. Summers responded to her call.

"Hello—Midge?" Irene spoke quickly. "Sorry to bother you at this late hour, but I was wondering—"

Connie stood beside her, trying to control her sniffles as she listened. But Irene's words and the pauses between them told their own story, and when at last she hung up and turned her anguished face to the light Connie started to cry again.

"You heard?" Irene said. "Bill's gone too." Then her voice broke. "Oh my God!" She rose. "What's keeping Howard so long?"

The answer came as a car screeched to a halt in the driveway and Irene opened the front door to admit her husband. The night wind was cold, but what really chilled her as he entered was the realization that Howard was alone.

"No sign of him," he muttered. "I covered everything for a half mile up and down, and there's not a kid out anywhere."

"There wouldn't be, at this hour." Irene nodded. "I know he's not at the Summerses', but maybe he and Bill stopped by somewhere else. I'm going to phone the Coopers and see—"

"Don't bother," Howard said. "I've just come from there. And before that I looked in on the Stuttmans and those new people, Higgins or whatever their name is. Their kids haven't come home either."

"But that's impossible! Do you realize it's past eleven-thirty?" She trembled, fighting the tears. "Where could they be?"

"We'll find out." Howard brushed past her, striding toward the phone. "I'm calling the police."

The grandfather's clock began to boom its message of midnight as potbellied Benjamin Franklin and little old Mrs. See peered into the parlor at the left of the front hallway.

"I'm glad we used candy this time," she said. "And that was a good idea of yours, giving money instead if the youngsters came to the door with their parents."

It was dark in the parlor and they had only a moment to stare through the shadows at the huddled forms lying motionless within.

"How many are there?" he said.

"Thirteen." She beamed at him as the chimes came to an end. "At least we won't be going hungry."

Sergeant Lichner kept his cool, but it wasn't easy. The station was like a madhouse, all those parents yelling and crying, and it took a team of four men just to question them and get some facts, instead of listening to wild guesses about kidnappers or crazies who put razor blades in Halloween candy.

But in the end he got it all together, using the statements to map out a route. Putting through some phone calls to establish where each child or group of children had last been seen, it turned out that everything must have happened somewhere within the area of one square block.

Then he called in backups and started out. There were four black-and-whites assigned to the search, each with its quota of parents, and each taking a single side of the block as they went from door to door asking questions.

On three sides the answers formed a pattern. Various youngsters had knocked on doors at various times, but all had been seen and accounted for.

Sergeant Lichner himself was in a fifth car, and to speed matters up he took one end of the block while the fourth car started at the other.

It wasn't until the two cars converged in the middle of the block to compare notes that he got an answer. Sid Olney pulled up and got out, shaking his head. "They were here, all right," he said. "Stopped at every house back there, right on up until around eleven. What did you find out, anything?"

Sergeant Lichner took a deep breath. "Same as you." He glanced at the house directly behind him. "Folks in the last place said the Esterhazy kid and the Summers boy were there late, almost eleven-thirty. What time did your people see them?"

Sid Olney shook his head. "They didn't." He shook his head. "That's funny."

But there was no mirth in his eyes, or the eyes of the parents as they stared at the spot where the trail ended—the space between the two

All Hallows' Eve

Halloween is a celebration of spooks and goblins, mysteries and magic. What is now called Halloween actually evolved from an ancient European holiday known as All Hallows' Eve: the day supernatural spirits were known to wander the earth. It began as the ancient Celtic festival of Samhain, which marked the moment when the veil between the living and the dead was lifted, and inhabitants of the two worlds could commune. For some 2000 years, October 31st meant bidding goodbye to summer, welcoming winter, and remembering the dead. Samhain marked the death of the old year and the birth of the next. It was a day of the dead, a night of magic and divination, a time when ghosts and lost souls roamed the land.

According to legend, every Samhain the souls of the dead were set free by the Lord of the Dead. It was believed that many of these spirits then roamed the natural world searching for bodies to possess. Families began dressing in scary disguises and noisily marching around their neighborhoods to scare away these immortal souls. This practice became the origin of the modern Halloween traditions of wearing costumes and committing harmless pranks.

So the next time you are choosing what to be for Halloween, remember all those spirits looking for a strong healthy body to inhabit, and pick a costume that is truly terrifying—it just might save your soul.

GHOSTLY EYEBALL GOO

A must-have for any Halloween party! Blindfold your guests before asking them to put their hands into this bowl of goop! When they feel those slimy wet grapes between their fingers, they'll think they're touching eyeballs for sure!

1 lb. red or green grapes
4 cups water
1 large box of Cherry Jello Powder
(8 servings size)

1. Peel the skin off of the grapes and set aside in a large Pyrex bowl.
2. In a medium size pot, over medium heat bring 2 cups water to a simmer. Add Jello and stir. Continue to simmer until consistency is completely smooth. Remove from heat, add 2 cups cold water, and pour over bowl of grapes. Stir well. Refrigerate for 3 hours or until Jello is firm.
3. Remove from refrigerator a few hours before the party and allow Jello mixture to sit at room temperature.

How To Counteract Spells

There's nothing worse than being cursed! Here are a few simple ways to counteract a nasty spell, even if you're the one who's been bewitched.

1. Place a penny in your pillowcase, add a piece of birch bark and a sprig of willow. Recite the following charm for a week each night before you go to bed and the curse will disappear:

> A lucky penny in my pillow,
> A piece of birch bark and some willow.
> I give these gifts to you my friend,
> So that this curse on me may end.

2. With adult supervision, take a wax figure of the witch or wizard who cast the spell and melt it in a pot. Dig a hole in the dirt at least two feet deep and pour in the hot wax. Bury it there and cover the fresh earth with mint and sage.

3. If you are fortunate enough to be there when the curse is cast upon you, extend one arm, spread all five fingers in front of your enemy's face and shout, "REVERSE THE CURSE!" The spell will bounce right off your hand and back onto the one who performed it.

VAMPIRES

Vampires first appeared in Slavic folktales about 1000 years ago. Plagued by disease and death—which were completely mysterious in those days—villagers blamed "corpses that traveled at night and sucked the blood from victims." This explanation for the troubles and, more importantly, being able to take a course of action against them, relieved anxiety in the community. Thus peasants eager to rid the village of this malevolence often dug up graves and dispatched those with signs of being a vampire by impaling the heart with a steak or beheading it. Furthermore, to keep the undead out of the house, garlic, religious symbols or exposure to daylight were thought to work.

Over the years vampires acquired various characteristics such as superhuman strength and speed, hypnotic mind control and inhuman stealth. As for looks, Bram Stoker's Dracula was a tall, older man with a long white moustache, pale, pointy ears and hairs in the center of his palms, while tuxedoed Bela Lugosi was a suave aristocrat. But the vampire's ability to shape-shift (mostly into bats or mist), is nowhere more stunning than its metamorphosis from, bloated, undead villagers to Tom Cruise and Brad Pitt.

THE CURSE OF THE
BURTON AGNES SKULL

When the Griffin family decided to build a new home on their Yorkshire lands in 1598, their three daughters took great interest in the project. Anne, in particular, followed every detail of constructing Burton Agnes Hall from start to finish, and grew very attached to the grand house after moving in.

One night, while returning from a visit to a neighbor, Anne was attacked on the road by a gang of thieves. She was struck in the head and, if not for her rescue by villagers who heard her screams, she would have died on the spot. She was brought home to the loving arms of her family, but the outlook was grim. Before dying, Anne begged her sisters to keep part of her in Burton Agnes Hall forever. In her final farewell, she asked them to have her skull buried within the walls of the house she had helped to build.

Anne died five days after the attack, and her family ignored her request by burying her—head and all—in the church graveyard. Soon, blood-curdling screams began to ring out in Burton Agnes Hall. No one could discover their source. Alarmed and chilled to the bone in fear, the sisters feared that the screams were a ghostly call from Anne to fulfill her dying wish. The family, with no other solution in sight, decided to dig up Anne's grave and obey her wishes. When the coffin was opened, the small group received another grisly shock: the body had not decayed, but the head had fallen off and lost every bit of hair and tissue, leaving only a bare skull. The Griffins took the skull home and the screams stopped.

All was well for many years, until the house was sold to another family who banished the skull from the hall. The screams returned, much to the horror of the new inhabitants. Again the skull was returned, and all was quiet once more. Later, a new owner hid the skull away within a wall and never told anyone where it was hidden. No one has found the skull's hiding place to this day, and the screams have not returned. Some people have seen Anne floating through the house in October, the month in which she was killed. They recognize the ghost as Anne, as it matches her portrait, which hangs in the home to this day.

THE JUDGE'S HOUSE

BY BRAM STOKER

When the time for his examination drew near, Malcolm Malcolmson made up his mind to go somewhere to read by himself. He packed a portmanteau with some clothes and all the books he required, and then took ticket for the first name on the local timetable which he did not know.

When at the end of three hours' journey he alighted at Benchurch, he felt satisfied that he had so far obliterated his tracks as to be sure of having a peaceful opportunity of pursuing his studies. He went straight to the one inn which the sleepy little place contained, and put up for the night. Malcolmson looked around the day after his arrival to try to find quarters more isolated than even so quiet an inn as "The good Traveller" afforded. There was only one place which took his fancy, and it certainly satisfied his wildest ideas regarding quiet; in fact, quiet was not the proper word to apply to it—desolation was the only term conveying any suitable idea of its isolation. It was an old rambling, heavy-built house of the Jacobean style, with heavy gables and windows, unusually small, and set higher than was customary in such houses, and was surrounded with a high brick wall, massively built. Indeed, on examination, it looked more like a fortified house than an ordinary dwelling. But all these things pleased Malcolmson. His joy was increased when he realized beyond doubt that it was not at present inhabited.

From the post office he got the name of the agent, who was rarely surprised at the application to rent a part of the old house. Mr. Carnford, the local lawyer and agent, was a genial old gentleman, and frankly confessed his delight at anyone being willing to live in the house. "To tell you the truth," said he, "I should be only too happy, on behalf of the owners, to let anyone have the house rent free for a term of years if only to accustom the people here to see it inhabited. It has been so long empty that some kind of absurd prejudice has grown up about it, and this can be best put down by its occupation—if only," he added with a sly glance at Malcolmson, "by a scholar like yourself, who wants it quiet for a time."

Malcolmson thought it needless to ask the agent about the "absurd prejudice"; he knew he would get more information, if he should require it, on that subject from other quarters. He paid his three months' rent, got a receipt, and the name of an old woman who would probably undertake to "do" for him, and came away with the keys in his pocket. He then went to the landlady of the inn, who was a cheerful and most kindly person, and asked her advice as to such stores and provisions as he would be likely to require. She threw up her hands in amazement when he told her where he was going to settle himself.

"Not in the Judge's House!" she said, and grew pale as she spoke. He explained the locality of the house, saying that he did not know its name.

When he had finished she answered, "It is the Judge's House sure enough." He asked her to tell him about the place. She told him that it was so called locally because it had been many years before—how long she could not say, as she was herself from another part of the country, but she thought it must have been a hundred years or more—the abode of a judge who was held in great terror on account of his harsh sentences and his hostility to prisoners at Assizes. As to what there was against the house itself she could not tell. She had often asked, but no one could inform her; but there was a general feeling that there was *something*, and for her own part she would not take all the money in Drinkwater's Bank and stay in the house an hour by herself. Then she apologized to Malcolmson for her disturbing talk.

"It is too bad of me, sir, and you—and a young gentleman, too— if you will pardon me saying it, going to live there all alone. If you were my boy you wouldn't sleep there a night, not if I had to go there myself and pull the big alarm bell that's on the roof!" The good creature was so manifestly in earnest, and was so kindly in her intentions, that Malcolmson, although amused, was touched.

He told her kindly how much he appreciated her interest in him, and added, "But, my dear Mrs. Witham, indeed you need not be concerned about me! A man who is reading for the Mathematical Tripos

has too much to think of to be disturbed by any of these mysterious 'somethings,' and his work is of too exact and prosaic a kind to allow of his having any corner in his mind for mysteries of any kind. Harmonical Progression, Permutations and Combinations, and Elliptic Functions have sufficient mysteries for me!" Mrs. Witham kindly undertook to see after his commissions, and he went himself to look for the old woman who had been recommended to him.

When he returned to the Judge's House with her, after an interval of a couple of hours, he found Mrs. Witham herself waiting with several men and boys carrying parcels, and an upholsterer's man with a bed in a cart. She was evidently curious to see the inside of the house; and though manifestly so afraid of the "somethings" that at the slightest sound she clutched on to Malcolmson, whom she never left for a moment, went over the whole place.

After his examination of the house, Malcolmson decided to take up his abode in the great dining room; and Mrs. Witham, with the aid of the charwoman, Mrs. Dempster, proceeded to arrange matters. When the hampers were brought in and unpacked, Malcolmson saw that with much kind forethought she had sent from her own kitchen sufficient provisions to last for a few days. Before going she expressed all sorts of kind wishes; and at the door turned and said, "And perhaps, sir, as the room is big and draughty it might be well to have one of those big screens put round your bed at night—though, truth to tell, I would die myself if I were to be so shut in with all kinds of—of 'things,' that put their heads round the sides, or over the top, and look on me!" The image which she had called up was too much for her nerves, and she fled incontinently.

Mrs. Dempster sniffed in a superior manner as the landlady disappeared, and remarked that for her own part she wasn't afraid of all the bogies in the kingdom. "I'll tell you what it is, sir," she said, "bogies is all kinds and sorts of things—except bogies! Rats and mice, and beetles; and creaky doors, and loose slates, and broken panes. Look at the wainscot of the room! It is old—hundreds of years old! Do you think there's no rats and beetles there! And do you imagine, sir, that you won't see none of them! Rats is bogies, I tell you, and bogies is rats; and don't you get to think anything else!" She set to work with her cleaning; and by nightfall, when Malcolmson returned from his walk he found the room swept and tidied, a fire burning in the old hearth, the lamp lit, and the table spread for supper with Mrs. Witham's excellent fare. "This is comfort, indeed," he said, as he rubbed his hands.

When he had finished his supper, he got out his books again, put fresh wood on the fire, trimmed his lamp, and set himself down to a spell of real hard work. He went on without a pause till about eleven o'clock, when he knocked off for a bit to fix his fire and lamp, and to make himself a cup of tea. He had always been a tea drinker, and during his college life had sat late at work and had taken tea late. The rest was a great luxury to him, and he enjoyed it with a sense of delicious, voluptuous ease. As he sipped his hot tea he revelled in the sense of isolation from his kind. Then it was that he began to notice for the first time what a noise the rats were making.

"Surely," he thought, "they cannot have been at it all the time I was reading. Had they been, I must have noticed it!" Presently, when the noise increased, he satisfied himself that it was really new. It was evident that at first the rats had been frightened at the presence of a stranger, and the light of fire and lamp; but that as the time went on they had grown bolder and were now disporting themselves as was their wont.

How busy they were! and hark to the strange noises! Up and down behind the old wainscot, over the ceiling and under the floor they raced, and gnawed, and scratched! Malcolmson smiled to himself as he recalled to mind the saying of Mrs. Dempster, "Bogies is rats, and rats is bogies!" The tea began to have its effect of intellectual and nervous stimulus; he saw with joy another long spell of work to be done before the night was past, and in the sense of security which it gave him, he allowed himself the luxury of a good look round the room. He took his lamp in one hand, and went all around, wondering that so quaint and beautiful an old house had been so long neglected. There were some old pictures on the walls, but they were coated so thick with dust and dirt that he could not distinguish any detail of them, though he held his lamp as high as he could over his head. Here and there as he went round, he saw some crack or hole blocked for a moment by the face of a rat with its bright eyes glittering in the light, but in an instant it was gone, and a squeak and a scamper followed.

The thing that most struck him, however, was the rope of the great alarm bell on the roof, which hung down in a corner of the room on the right-hand side of the fireplace. He pulled up close to the hearth a great high-backed carved oak chair, and sat down to his last cup of tea. When this was done he made up the fire, and went back to his work sitting at the corner of the table, having the fire to his left. For a while the rats disturbed him somewhat with their perpetual scampering, but he got accustomed to the noise, and he became so immersed in his work that everything in the world, except the problem which he was trying to solve, passed away from him.

He suddenly looked up, his problem was still unsolved, and there was in the air that sense of the hour before dawn, which is so dread to doubtful life. The noise of the rats had ceased. Indeed it seemed to him that it must have ceased but lately and that it was the sudden cessation which had disturbed him. As he looked, he started in spite of his *sang froid.*

There on the great high-backed carved oak chair by the right side of the fireplace sat an enormous rat, steadily glaring at him with baleful eyes. He made a motion to it as though to hunt it away, but it did not stir. Then he made the motion of throwing something. Still it did not stir, but showed its great white teeth angrily, and its cruel eyes shone in the lamplight with an added vindictiveness.

Malcolmson felt amazed, and seizing the poker from the hearth ran at it to kill it. Before, however, he could strike it, the rat, with a squeak that sounded like the concentration of hate, jumped upon the floor, and, running up the rope of the alarm bell, disappeared in the darkness. Instantly, strange to say, the noisy scampering of the rats in the wainscot began again.

By this time Malcolmson's mind was quite off the problem; and as a shrill cock-crow outside told him of the approach of morning, he went to bed and to sleep.

He slept so sound that he was not even waked by Mrs. Dempster coming in to make up his room. It was only when she had tidied up the place and got his breakfast ready and tapped on the screen which closed in his bed that he woke. He was a little tired still after his night's hard work, but a strong cup of tea soon freshened him up, and, taking his book, he went out for his morning walk. On his return he looked in to see Mrs. Witham and to thank her for her kindness. When she saw him coming through the bay window of her sanctum, she came out to meet him and asked him in.

She looked at him searchingly and shook her head as she said, "You must not overdo it, sir. You are paler this morning than you should be. Too late hours and too hard work on the brain isn't good for any man! But tell me, sir, how did you pass the night? But, my heart! sir, I was glad when Mrs. Dempster told me this morning that you were all right and sleeping sound when she went in."

"Oh, I was all right," he answered, smiling, "the 'somethings' didn't worry me, as yet. Only the rats; and they had a circus, I tell you, all over the place. There was one wicked looking old devil that sat up on my own chair by the fire, and wouldn't go till I took the poker to him, and then he ran up the rope of the alarm bell and got to somewhere up the wall or the ceiling—I couldn't see where, it was so dark."

"Mercy on us," said Mrs. Witham, "an old devil, and sitting on a chair by the fireside! Take care, sir! take care! There's many a true word spoken in jest."

"How do you mean? 'Pon my word I don't understand."

"An old devil! The old devil, perhaps. There! sir, you needn't laugh," for Malcolmson had broken into a hearty peal. "You young folks thinks it easy to laugh at things that makes older ones shudder. Never mind, sir! never mind! Please God, you'll laugh all the time. It's what I wish you myself!" and the good lady beamed all over in sympathy with his enjoyment, her fears gone for a moment.

"Oh, forgive me!" said Malcolmson presently. "Don't think me rude; but the idea was too much for me—that the old devil himself was on the chair last night!" And at the thought he laughed again. Then he went home to dinner.

This evening the scampering of the rats began earlier; indeed it

had been going on before his arrival, and only ceased whilst his presence, by its freshness, disturbed them. After dinner he began to work as before. Tonight the rats disturbed him more than they had done on the previous night. Now and again as they disturbed him Malcolmson made a sound to frighten them, smiting the table with his hand or giving a fierce "Hsh, hsh," so that they fled straightway to their holes.

And so the early part of the night wore on; and despite the noise Malcolmson got more and more immersed in his work.

All at once he stopped, as on the previous night, being overcome by a sudden sense of silence. There was not the faintest sound of gnaw, or scratch, or squeak. The silence was as of the grave. He remembered the odd occurrence of the previous night, and instinctively he looked at the chair standing close by the fireside. And then a very odd sensation thrilled through him.

There, on the great old high-backed carved oak chair beside the fireplace sat the same enormous rat, steadily glaring at him with baleful eyes.

Instinctively he took the nearest thing to his hand, a book of logarithms, and flung it at it. The book was badly aimed and the rat did not stir, so again the poker performance of the previous night was repeated; and again the rat, being closely pursued, fled up the rope of the alarm bell.

Strangely too, the departure of this rat was instantly followed by the renewal of the noise made by the general rat community. On this occasion, as on the previous one, Malcolmson could not see at what part of the room the rat disappeared, for the green shade of his lamp left the upper part of the room in darkness, and the fire had burned low.

On looking at his watch he found it was close on midnight; and he made up his fire and made himself his nightly pot of tea. He had got through a good spell of work, and thought himself entitled to a cigarette; so he sat on the great carved oak chair before the fire and enjoyed it. Whilst smoking he began to think that he would like to know where the rat disappeared to, for he had certain ideas for the morrow not entirely disconnected with a rat trap. Accordingly he lit another lamp and placed it so that it would shine well into the right-hand corner of the wall by the fireplace. Then he got all the books he had with him, and placed them handy to throw at the vermin. Finally he lifted the rope of the alarm bell and placed the end of it on the table, fixing the extreme end under the lamp. As he handled it he could not help noticing how pliable it was, especially for so strong a rope, and one not in use. "You could hang a man with it," he thought to himself.

When his preparations were made he looked around, and said complacently, "There now, my friend, I think we shall learn something of you this time!" He began his work again, and though as before somewhat disturbed at first by the noise of the rats, soon lost himself in his propositions and problems.

Again he was called to his immediate surroundings suddenly. This time it might not have been the sudden silence only which took his attention; there was a slight movement of the rope, and the lamp moved. Without stirring, he looked to see if his pile of books was within range, and then cast his eye along the rope. As he looked he saw the great rat drop from the rope on the oak armchair and sit there glaring at him. He raised a book in his right hand, and taking careful aim, flung it at the rat. The latter, with a quick movement, sprang aside and dodged the missile. He then took another book, and a third, and flung them one after another at the rat, but each time unsuccessfully. At last, as he stood with a book poised in his hand to throw, the rat squeaked and seemed to be afraid. This made Malcolmson more than ever eager to strike, and the book flew and struck the rat a resounding blow. It gave a terrified squeak, and turning on its pursuer a look of terrible malevolence, ran up the chairback and made a great jump to the rope of the alarm bell and ran up it like lightning. The lamp rocked under the sudden strain, but it was a heavy one and did not topple over. Malcolmson kept his eyes on the rat, and saw it by the light of the second lamp leap to a molding of the wainscot and disappear through a hole in one of the great pictures which hung on the wall, obscured and invisible through its coating of dirt and dust.

"I shall look up my friend's habitation in the morning," said the student, as he went over to collect his books. "The third picture from the fireplace; I shall not forget." He picked up the books one by one, commenting on them as he lifted them. "*Conic Sections* he does not mind, nor *Cycloidal Oscillations*, nor the *Principia*, nor *Quaternions*, nor *Thermodynamics*. Now for the book that fetched him!"

Malcolmson took it up and looked at it. As he did so he started, and a sudden pallor overspread his face. He looked round uneasily and shivered slightly, as he murmured to himself, "The Bible my mother gave me! What an odd coincidence." He sat down to work again, and the rats in the wainscot renewed their gambols. They did not disturb him, however; somehow their presence gave him a sense of companionship. But he could not attend to his work, and after striving to master the subject on which he was engaged, gave it up in despair, and went to bed as the first streak of dawn stole in through the eastern window.

He slept heavily but uneasily, and dreamed much; and when Mrs. Dempster woke him late in the morning he seemed ill at ease, and for a few minutes did not seem to realize exactly where he was. His first request rather surprised the servant.

"Mrs. Dempster, when I am out today, I wish you would get the steps and dust or wash those pictures—specially that one, the third from the fireplace—I want to see what they are."

Late in the afternoon Malcolmson worked at his books in the shaded walk, and the cheerfulness of the previous day came back to him as the day wore on, and he found that his reading was progressing well. He had worked out to a satisfactory conclusion all the problems which had as yet baffled him, and it was in a state of jubilation that he paid a visit to Mrs. Witham at "The Good Traveler." He found a stranger in the cozy sitting-room with the landlady, who was introduced to him as Dr. Thornhill. She was not quite at ease, and this, combined with the Doctor's plunging at once into a series of questions, made Malcolmson come to the conclusion that his presence was not an accident. So without preliminary he said, "Dr. Thornhill, I shall with pleasure answer you any question you may choose to ask me if you will answer me one question first."

The Doctor seemed surprised, but he smiled and answered at once. "Done! What is it?"

"Did Mrs. Witham ask you to come here and advise me?"

Dr. Thornhill for a moment was taken aback, and Mrs. Witham got fiery red and turned away; but the Doctor was a frank and ready man, and he answered at once and openly. "She did, but she didn't intend you to know it. She told me that she did not like the idea of your being in that house all by yourself, and that she thought you took too much strong tea. In fact, she wants me to advise you, if possible, to give up the tea and the very late hours. I was a keen student in my time, so I suppose I may take the liberty of a college man, and without offense, advise you not quite as a stranger."

Malcolmson with a smile held out his hand. "Shake! as they say in America," he said. "I must thank you for your kindness and Mrs. Witham too, and your kindness deserves a return on my part. I promise to take no more strong tea—no tea at all till you let me—and I shall go

to bed tonight at one o'clock at latest. Will that do?"

"Capital," said the Doctor. "Now tell us all that you noticed in the old house," and so Malcolmson, then and there, told in minute detail all that had happened in the last two nights. He was interrupted every now and then by some exclamation from Mrs. Witham, till finally when he told of the episode of the Bible the landlady's pent-up emotions found vent in a shriek; and it was not till a stiff glass of brandy and water had been administered that she grew composed again.

Dr. Thornhill listened with a face of growing gravity, and when the narrative was complete and Mrs. Witham had been restored he asked, "The rat always went up the rope of the alarm bell?"

"Always."

"I suppose you know," said the Doctor after a pause, "what the rope is?"

"No!"

"It is," said the Doctor slowly, "the very rope which the hangman used for all the victims of the Judge's judicial rancor!" Here he was interrupted by another scream from Mrs. Witham, and steps had to be taken for her recovery. Malcolmson having looked at his watch, and found that it was close to his dinner hour, had gone home before her complete recovery.

When Mrs. Witham was herself again she almost assailed the Doctor with angry questions as to what he meant by putting such horrible ideas into the poor man's mind.

Dr. Thornhill replied, "My dear madam, I had a distinct purpose in it! I wanted to draw his attention to the bell rope, and to fix it there. It may be that he is in a highly overwrought state, and has been studying too much, although I am bound to say that he seems as sound and healthy a young man, mentally and bodily, as ever I saw—but then the rats—and that suggestion of the devil." The doctor shook his head and went on. "I would have offered to go and stay the first night with him but that I felt sure it would have been a cause of offense. He may get in the night some strange fright or hallucination; and if he does, I want him to pull that rope. All alone as he is it will give us warning, and we may reach him in time to be of service. Do not be alarmed if Benchurch gets a surprise before morning."

"Oh, Doctor, what do you mean? What do you mean?"

"I mean this; that possibly—nay, more probably—we shall hear the great alarm bell from the Judge's House tonight," and the Doctor made about as effective an exit as could be thought of.

When Malcolmson arrived home he found that it was a little after his usual time, and Mrs. Dempster had gone away. For a few minutes after his entrance the noise of the rats ceased; but so soon as they

became accustomed to his presence they began again. He was glad to
hear them, for he felt once more the feeling of companionship in their
noise, and his mind ran back to the strange fact that they only ceased to
manifest themselves when that other—the great rat with the baleful
eyes—came upon the scene. The reading lamp only was lit, and its green
shade kept the ceiling and the upper part of the room in darkness, so
that the cheerful light from the hearth, spreading over the floor and
shining on the white cloth laid over the end of the table, was warm and
cheery. Malcolmson sat down to his dinner with a good appetite and a
buoyant spirit. After his dinner and a cigarette he sat steadily down to
work, determined not to let anything disturb him.

For an hour or so he worked all right, and then his thoughts
began to wander from his books. The actual circumstances around him,
the calls on his physical attention, and his nervous susceptibility were
not to be denied. By this time the wind had become a gale, and the gale
a storm. Even the great alarm bell on the roof must have felt the
force of the wind, for the rope rose and fell slightly, as though
the bell were moved a little from time to time, and the limber
rope fell on the oak floor with a hard and hollow sound.

As Malcolmson listened to it he bethought himself of
the doctor's words, "It is the rope which the hangman used for
the victims of the Judge's judicial rancour," and he went over to
the corner of the fireplace and took it in his hand to look at it. There
seemed a sort of deadly interest in it, and as he stood there he lost

himself for a moment in speculation as to who these victims were, and the grim wish of the Judge to have such a ghastly relic ever under his eyes. As he stood there the swaying of the bell on the roof still lifted the rope now and again; but presently there came a new sensation—a sort of tremor in the rope, as though something was moving along it.

Looking up instinctively Malcolmson saw the great rat coming slowly down towards him, glaring at him steadily. He dropped the rope and started back with a muttered curse, and the rat turning ran up the rope again and disappeared, and at the same instant, Malcolmson became conscious that the noise of the rats, which had ceased for a while, began again.

All this set him thinking, and it occurred to him that he had not investigated the lair of the rat or looked at the pictures, as he had intended. He lit the other lamp, and, holding it up, went and stood opposite the third picture from the fireplace on the right-hand side where he had seen the rat disappear on the previous night.

At the first glance he started back so suddenly that he almost dropped the lamp, and a deadly pallor overspread his face. But he was young and plucky, and pulled himself together, and after the pause of a few seconds stepped forward again, raised the lamp, and examined the picture which had been dusted and washed, and now stood out clearly.

It was of a judge dressed in his robes of scarlet and ermine. His face was strong and merciless, evil, crafty, and vindictive, with a sensual mouth, hooked nose of ruddy colour, and shaped like the beak of a bird

of prey. The eyes were of peculiar brilliance and with a terribly malignant expression. As he looked at them, Malcolmson grew cold, for he
saw there the very counterpart of the eyes of the great rat. The lamp
almost fell from his hand, he saw the rat with its baleful eyes peering
out through the hole in the corner of the picture, and noted the sudden
cessation of the noise of the other rats. However, he pulled himself
together, and went on with his examination of the picture.

The Judge was seated in a great high-backed carved oak chair, on
the right-hand side of a great stone fireplace where, in the corner, a rope
hung down from the ceiling, its end lying coiled on the floor. With a
feeling of something like horror, Malcolmson recognized the scene of
the room as it stood, and gazed around in an awe struck manner as
though he expected to find some strange presence behind him. Then he
looked over to the corner of the fireplace—and with a loud cry he let
the lamp fall from his hand.

There, in the Judge's armchair, with the rope hanging behind, sat
the rat with the Judge's baleful eyes, now intensified and with a fiendish
leer. Save for the howling of the storm without there was silence.

The fallen lamp recalled Malcolmson to himself. Fortunately it
was of metal, and so the oil was not spilt. However, the practical need
of attending to it settled at once his nervous apprehensions. When he
had turned it out, he wiped his brow and thought for a moment.

"This will not do," he said to himself. "If I go on like this I shall
become a crazy fool. This must stop! I promised the Doctor I would
not take tea. Faith, he was pretty right! My nerves must have been get-

ting into a queer state. Funny I did not notice it. I never felt better in my life. However, it is all right now, and I shall not be such a fool again." Then he mixed himself a good stiff glass of brandy and water and resolutely sat down to his work.

It was nearly an hour when he looked up from his book, disturbed by the sudden stillness. Malcolmson listened attentively, and presently heard a thin, squeaking noise, very faint. It came from the corner of the room where the rope hung down, and he thought it was the creaking of the rope on the floor as the swaying of the bell raised and lowered it. Looking up, however, he saw in the dim light the great rat clinging to the rope and gnawing it. The rope was already nearly gnawed through—he could see the lighter colour where the strands were laid bare. As he looked the job was completed, and the severed end of the rope fell clattering on the oaken floor, whilst for an instant the great rat remained like a knob or tassel at the end of the rope, which now began to sway to and fro. Malcolmson felt for a moment another pang of terror as he thought that now the possibility of calling the outer world to his assistance was cut off, but an intense anger took its place, and seizing the book he was reading he hurled it at the rat. The blow was well aimed, but before the missile could reach it the rat dropped off and struck the floor with a soft thud. Malcolmson instantly rushed over towards it, but it darted away and disappeared in the darkness of the shadows of the room. Malcolmson felt that his work was over for the night, and determined then and there to vary the monotony of the proceedings by a hunt for the rat. From where he stood, Malcolmson saw right opposite to him the third picture on the wall from the right of the fireplace. He rubbed his eyes in surprise, and then a great fear began to come upon him.

In the center of the picture was a great irregular patch of brown canvas, as fresh as when it was stretched on the frame. The background was as before, with chair and chimney-corner and rope, but the figure of the Judge had disappeared.

Malcolmson, almost in a chill of horror, turned slowly round, and then he began to shake and tremble like a man in a palsy. His strength seemed to have left him, and he was incapable of action or movement, hardly even of thought. He could only see and hear.

There, on the great high-backed carved oak chair sat the Judge in his robes of scarlet and ermine, with his baleful eyes glaring vindictively, and a smile of triumph on the resolute, cruel mouth, as he lifted with his hands a *black cap*. Malcolmson felt as if the blood was running from his heart, as one does in moments of prolonged suspense. There was a singing in his ears. Without, he could hear the roar and howl of the tempest, and through it, swept on the storm, came the striking of midnight by the great chimes in the marketplace. He stood for a space of time that seemed to him endless, still as a statue and with wide-open, horror-struck eyes, breathless. As the clock struck, so the smile of triumph on the Judge's face intensified, and at the last stroke of midnight he placed the black cap on his head.

Slowly and deliberately the Judge rose from his chair and picked up the piece of rope of the alarm bell which lay on the floor, drew it through his hands as if he enjoyed the touch, and then deliberately began to know one end of it, fashioning it into a noose. Then he began to move along the table on the opposite side to Malcolmson, keeping his eyes on him until he had passed him, when with a quick movement he stood in front of the door. Malcolmson then began to feel that he was trapped, and tried to think of what he should do. There was some fascination in the Judge's eyes, which he never took off him, and he had, perforce, to look. He saw the Judge approach—still keeping between him and the door—and raise the noose and throw it towards him as if to entangle him. With a great effort he made a quick movement to one side, and saw the rope fall beside him, and heard it strike the oaken floor. Again the Judge raised the noose and tried to ensnare him, ever keeping his baleful eyes fixed on him, and each time by a mighty effort the student just managed to evade it. So this went on for many times, the Judge seeming never discouraged nor discomposed at failure, but playing as a cat does with a mouse. At last, in despair which had reached its climax, Malcolmson cast a quick glance round him. The lamp seemed to have blazed up, and there was a fairly good light in the room. At the many rat-holes and in the chinks and crannies of the wainscot he saw the rats' eyes; and this aspect, that was purely physical, gave him a gleam of comfort. He looked around and saw that the rope of the great alarm bell was laden with rats. Every inch of it was covered with them, and more and more were pouring through the small circular hole in the ceiling whence it emerged, so that with their weight the bell was beginning to sway. Hark! it had swayed till the clapper had touched

the bell. The sound was but a tiny one, but the bell was only beginning
to sway, and it would increase.

At the sound the Judge, who had been keeping his eyes fixed on
Malcolmson, looked up, and a scowl of diabolical anger overspread his
face. A dreadful peal of thunder broke overhead as he raised the rope
again, whilst the rats kept running up and down the rope as though
working against time. This time, instead of throwing it, he drew close
to his victim, and held open the noose as he approached. As he came
closer there seemed something paralyzing in his very presence, and
Malcolmson stood rigid as a corpse. He felt the Judge's icy fingers touch his throat as he adjusted the rope. Then the Judge,
taking the rigid form of the student in his arms, carried him
over and placed him standing in the oak chair, and stepping up
beside him, put his hand up and caught the end of the swaying rope of the alarm bell. As he raised his hand the rats fled
squeaking, and disappeared through the hole in the ceiling.
Taking the end of the noose which was round Malcolmson's
neck he tied it to the hanging bell-rope, and then descending, pulled away the chair.

When the alarm bell of the Judge's House began to sound a
crowd soon assembled. They knocked loudly at the door, but there was
no reply. Then they burst in the door, and poured into the great dining
room, the Doctor at the head. There at the end of the rope of the great
alarm bell hung the body of the student, and on the face of the Judge
in the picture was a malignant smile.

Houdini

The great Harry Houdini! We've all heard of this amazing magician and master escape artist. But who was the man behind the spectacle?

Harry Houdini was not born a great magician. In fact, he wasn't even born Harry Houdini! His real name was Ehrich Weiss. The son of two poor Hungarian immigrants, he adopted the name Houdini when, as a seventeen-year-old boy, he read the memoirs of Robert Houdin, a famous master of deception. Inspired by Houdin's story, Ehrich spontaneously committed himself to a life of illusion, and changed his name to Harry Houdini.

Like many magicians, the young Houdini started out with complicated card tricks. But it wasn't long before he discovered his talent for escaping handcuffs and other complex restraints. Although no one knows how Houdini accomplished such feats, his slight build and small hands certainly contributed to his unusual abilities. His claim that there was no restraint from which he could not escape intrigued and excited the public. Before long he had wowed American audiences with his sensational escapes from prisons, straightjackets, and handcuffs. But his greatest feats still lay ahead. . .

In 1900, Houdini sailed for Europe. London was considered to be heart of the performing arts and Houdini was determined to make his name there. He wasted little time beginning his meteoric rise to fame. One of his most notorious public escapes occurred in 1904. A British newspaper challenged Houdini to escape a specially designed pair of cuffs with six sets of locks. He succeeded in just over an hour, astounding more than four thousand spectators who had gathered to watch. Houdini traveled throughout Europe accepting any escape challenge no matter how complicated or death-defying. Whether suspended in mid-air, thrown off a bridge, or submerged underwater, Houdini successfully executed his dangerous escapes every time. During the following years he would release himself from sealed crates, shackles and chains, locked water cans—even the carcass of an enormous sea monster!

By the time of his death in 1926, the miraculous Harry Houdini had become the most famous entertainer of his kind. Remembered by the history books as a great adventurer and the ultimate underdog, Houdini remains an inspiration to young entertainers throughout the world.

CANDLES

When we think of séances, witches, fortune-tellers, haunted houses, or even Halloween, we think of candles. Candles are shrouded in mystery and superstition.

Beware the candle that blows out during a ceremony. It's a warning that evil is near. Three lit candles in a row bring bad luck. Quickly blow one out. Light a candle inside a jack-o'-lantern on Halloween to guard against evil spirits lurking about. If you look into a mirror by candlelight you may find the souls of the deceased. There's even a "corpse candle," which reveals the unusual presence of a small flame floating through the night air, believed to be a lost soul. Such a sight is considered an omen of death (understood by some to predict the death of the person witnessing the event).

Spooked? Remember, a candle's magic is not totally out of your control. Try using a pink candle against evil spirits, a red candle to bring love your way, or a black candle to put a curse on someone. For secrecy, it is believed that a candle in the hand of a dead man will not be seen by anyone but those who placed it there.

THE CURSE OF
KING TUT'S TOMB

For centuries, thieves broke into the tombs in Egypt's Valley of the Kings and ran off with gold and treasures. Modern-day archeologist Howard Carter was certain that one untouched tomb remained to be found—the final resting place of King Tutankhamon. The mysterious young Pharaoh, who reigned more than 3,300 years ago, died at the age of 18 and his tomb had never been found. For 30 years, Carter was obsessed in his search, but by 1922 his luck was running out. Lord Carnarvon, Carter's wealthy friend who funded his digs in the desert sands, had lost a fortune and didn't want to spend another dime. But Carter begged for one last chance, and he got it. He started digging in the last unexplored part of the Valley, and in November of 1922 uncovered a descending staircase. Frantic with excitement, Carter cabled Lord Carnarvon to fly down from England and join him in uncovering the tomb.

On November 26, 1922, Carter scraped a hole through the doorway to King Tutankhamon's tomb and lit a candle at the opening. Carnarvon stood beside him, restless for the news. "Can you see anything?" Carnarvon asked anxiously. "Yes," said Carter, barely able to speak, "wonderful things. . . ." Over the next few days they broke through the sealed doors and found rooms filled with gold statues, furniture, jewelry, and other priceless objects. Carter and Carnarvon also found a frightening message on a clay tablet. They swiftly hid it away, fearing the Egyptian workers would flee if they learned of it. The inscription was a warning and a curse:

DEATH WILL SLAY WITH HIS WINGS WHOEVER DISTURBS THE PEACE OF THE PHARAOH

King Tut's tomb soon proved to be the greatest archeological discovery of all time. The curse—which reached the newspapers after Carnarvon sold the story—became the most famous in history as headlines around the world announced "The Curse of the Pharaohs." The curse's first victim was Lord Carnarvon, who died of an unknown disease just five months after the discovery. An American journalist who helped unseal the tomb fell into a coma and died shortly after Carnarvon. A friend of Carnarvon came to visit the tomb and died the next day. A radiologist who took x-rays of King Tut's mummy died after returning to England. The death toll continued to climb, and by 1929 the curse had claimed 22 lives. Oddly, Howard Carter survived the curse and died of natural causes in 1939 at the age of 64.

BAKED APPLES

6 medium-sized apples
1/4 cup granulated sugar
1/2 cup brown sugar
6 tablespoons butter
3 teaspoons ground cinnamon

1. Preheat oven to 350°F.
2. In a small bowl, mix together brown and granulated sugars. Add butter and cream together.
3. Core apples, but do not cut all the way through. Place them in a baking dish filled with half an inch of water.
4. Fill each apple with three tablespoons of sugar and butter mixture.
5. Sprinkle 1/2 teaspoon of cinnamon on top of each apple.
6. Bake 15-20 minutes or until apples are tender.
7. Serve warm with vanilla ice cream.

Serves six

If You See a Fairy Ring
by Anonymous

If you see a fairy ring
In a field of grass,
Very lightly step around,
Tiptoe as you pass;
Last night fairies frolicked there,
And they're sleeping somewhere near.

If you see a tiny fairy
Lying fast asleep,
Shut your eyes and run away,
Do not stay to peep;
And be sure you never tell,
Or you'll break a fairy spell.

A FLYING EGG

With a puff of breath, you can send an egg flying out of one glass and into another.

The secret of this trick is to use a hollow, lightweight egg. To prepare the egg, puncture a tiny hole on each end with a needle. Stick the needle deep into one of the holes and move it around to break up the yoke. Standing over a bowl or the sink, put your mouth over one of the holes and blow. Keep blowing, forcefully, until the egg has completely drained out the opposite hole. Then hold the egg under running water to rinse it out.

Place two short glasses side by side, and put the egg into one of them. Handle the egg as if its heavier than it really is. Stand close to the glass holding the egg and blow along the inside wall, next to the egg. The egg will jump out and land into the other glass.

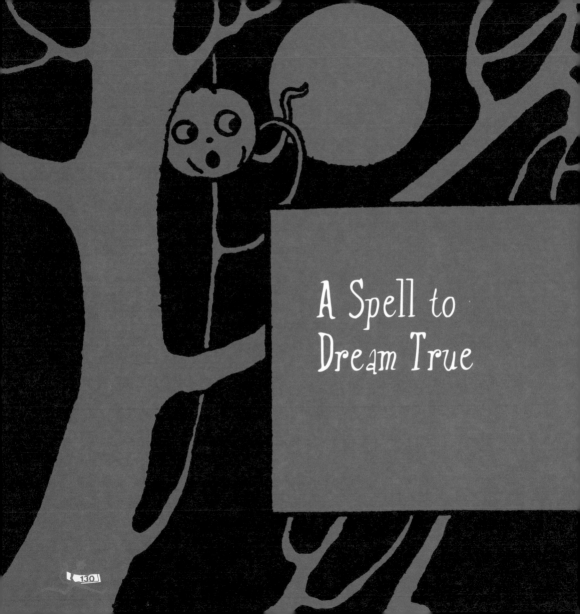

A Spell to
Dream True

It is well known among modern witches and sorcerers that dreams
are useful tools for foretelling the future. To inspire psychic
dreams, stuff your pillow with the leaves of the weed-like
mugwort plant. Using this dream pillow to inspire prophecy dates
back to ancient magical times. Always sleep alone when using a
Mugwort pillow and keep a pad and pencil handy to jot down your
visions as soon as you wake. If you cannot gather enough of the
herb to fill your pillow, just a few dried leaves burned as
incense should do the trick quite nicely.

A GHOST STORY

BY MARK TWAIN

I took a large room, far up Broadway, in a huge old building whose upper stories had been wholly unoccupied for years, until I came. The place had long been given up to dust and cobwebs, to solitude and silence. I seemed groping among the tombs and invading the privacy of the dead, that first night I climbed up to my quarters. For the first time in my life a superstitious dread came over me; and as I turned a dark angle of the stairway and an invisible cobweb swung its slazy woof in my face and clung there, I shuddered as one who had encountered a phantom.

I was glad enough when I reached my room and locked out the mould and the darkness. A cheery fire was burning in the grate, and I sat down before it with a comforting sense of relief. For two hours I sat there, thinking of bygone times; recalling old scenes, and summoning half-forgotten faces out of the mists of the past; listening, in fancy, to voices that long ago grew silent for all time, and to once familiar songs that nobody sings now. And as my reverie softened down to a sadder and sadder pathos, the shrieking of the winds outside softened to a wail, the angry beating of the rain against the panes diminished to a tranquil patter, and one by one the noises in the street subsided, until the hurrying foot-steps of the last belated straggler died away in the distance and left no sound behind.

The fire had burned low. A sense of loneliness crept over me. I arose and undressed, moving on tiptoe about the room, doing stealthily what I had to do, as if I were environed by sleeping enemies whose slumbers it would be fatal to break. I covered up in bed, and lay listening to the rain and wind and the faint creaking of distant shutters, till they lulled me to sleep.

I slept profoundly, but how long I do not know. All at once I found myself awake, and filled with a shuddering expectancy. All was still. All but my own heart—I could hear it beat. Presently the bed-clothes began to slip away slowly toward the foot of the bed, as if some one were pulling them! I could not stir; I could not speak. Still the blankets slipped deliberately away, till my breast was uncovered. Then with a great effort I seized them and drew them over my head. I waited, listened, waited. Once more that steady pull began, and once more I lay torpid a century of dragging seconds till my breast was naked again. At last I roused my energies and snatched the covers back to their place and held them with a strong grip. I waited. By and by I felt a faint tug, and took a fresh grip. The tug strengthened to a steady strain—it grew stronger and stronger. My hold parted, and for the third time the blankets slid away. I groaned. An answering groan came from the foot of the bed! Beaded drops of sweat stood upon my forehead. I was more dead than alive. Presently I heard a heavy footstep in my room—the step of an elephant, it seemed to me—it was not like anything human. But it was moving FROM me—there was relief in that. I heard it approach the door—pass out without moving bolt or lock—and wander away among the dismal corridors, straining the floors and joists till they creaked again as it passed—and then silence reigned once more.

When my excitement had calmed, I said to myself, "This is a dream—simply a hideous dream." And so I lay thinking it over until I convinced myself that it WAS a dream, and then a comforting laugh relaxed my lips and I was happy again. I got up and struck a light; and when I found that the locks and bolts were just as I had left them, another soothing laugh welled in my heart and rippled from my lips. I took my pipe and lit it, and was just sitting down before the fire, when—down went the pipe out of my nerveless fingers, the blood forsook my cheeks, and my placid breathing was cut short with a gasp! In the ashes on the hearth, side by side with my own bare footprint, was another, so vast that in comparison mine was but an infant's! Then I had HAD a visitor, and the elephant tread was explained.

I put out the light and returned to bed, palsied with fear. I lay a long time, peering into the darkness, and listening. Then I heard a grating noise overhead, like the dragging of a heavy body across the floor; then the throwing down of the body, and the shaking of my windows in response to the concussion. In distant parts of the building I heard the muffled slamming of doors. I heard, at intervals, stealthy footsteps

creeping in and out among the corridors, and up and down the stairs. Sometimes these noises approached my door, hesitated, and went away again. I heard the clanking of chains faintly, in remote passages, and listened while the clanking grew nearer—while it wearily climbed the stairways, marking each move by the loose surplus of chain that fell with an accented rattle upon each succeeding step as the goblin that bore it advanced. I heard muttered sentences; half-uttered screams that seemed smothered violently; and the swish of invisible garments, the rush of invisible wings. Then I became conscious that my chamber was invaded—that I was not alone. I heard sighs and breathings about my

bed, and mysterious whisperings. Three little spheres of soft phosphorescent light appeared on the ceiling directly over my head, clung and glowed there a moment, and then dropped—two of them upon my face and one upon the pillow. They spattered, liquidly, and felt warm. Intuition told me they had turned to gouts of blood as they fell—I needed no light to satisfy myself of that. Then I saw pallid faces, dimly luminous, and white uplifted hands, floating bodiless in the air— floating a moment and then disappearing. The whispering ceased, and the voices and the sounds, and a solemn stillness followed. I waited and listened. I felt that I must have light or die. I was weak with fear. I slowly raised myself toward a sitting posture, and my face came in contact with a clammy hand! All strength went from me apparently, and I fell back like a stricken invalid. Then I heard the rustle of a garment—it seemed to pass to the door and go out.

When everything was still once more, I crept out of bed, sick and feeble, and lit the gas with a hand that trembled as if it were aged with a hundred years. The light brought some little cheer to my spirits. I sat down and fell into a dreamy contemplation of that great footprint in the ashes. By and by its outlines began to waver and grow dim. I glanced up and the broad gas flame was slowly wilting away. In the same moment I heard that elephantine tread again. I noted its approach, nearer and nearer, along the musty halls, and dimmer and dimmer the light waned. The tread reached my very door and paused—the light had dwindled to a sickly blue, and all things about me lay in a spectral twilight. The door did not open, and yet I felt a faint gust of air fan my cheek, and presently was conscious of a huge, cloudy presence before me. I watched it with fascinated eyes. A pale glow stole over the Thing; gradually its cloudy folds took shape—an arm appeared, then legs, then a body, and last a great sad face looked out of the vapor. Stripped of its filmy housings, naked, muscular and comely, the majestic Cardiff Giant loomed above me!

All my misery vanished—for a child might know that no harm could come with that benignant countenance. My cheerful spirits returned at once, and in sympathy with them the gas flamed up brightly again. Never a lonely outcast was so glad to welcome company as I was to greet the friendly giant. I said:

"Why, is it nobody but you? Do you know, I have been scared to death for the last two or three hours? I am most honestly glad to see you. I wish I had a chair—Here, here, don't try to sit down in that thing!

But it was too late. He was in it before I could stop him, and down he went—I never saw a chair shiver so in my life.

"Stop, stop, You'll ruin ev—"

Too late again. There was another crash, and another chair was resolved into its original elements.

"Confound it, haven't you got any judgment at all? Do you want to ruin all the furniture on the place? Here, here, you petrified fool—"

But it was no use. Before I could arrest him he had sat down on the bed, and it was a melancholy ruin.

"Now what sort of a way is that to do? First you come lumbering about the place bringing a legion of vagabond goblins along with you to worry me to death, and then when I overlook an indelicacy of costume which would not be tolerated anywhere by cultivated people except in a respectable theater, and not even there if the nudity were of YOUR sex, you repay me by wrecking all the furniture you can find to sit down on. And why will you? You damage yourself as much as you do me. You have broken off the end of your spinal column, and littered up the floor with chips of your hams till the place looks like a marble yard. You ought to be ashamed of yourself—you are big enough to know better."

"Well, I will not break any more furniture. But what am I to do? I have not had a chance to sit down for a century." And the tears came into his eyes.

"Poor devil," I said, "I should not have been so harsh with you. And you are an orphan, too, no doubt. But sit down on the floor here— nothing else can stand your weight—and besides, we cannot be sociable with you away up there above me; I want you down where I can perch on this high counting-house stool and gossip with you face to face."

So he sat down on the floor, and lit a pipe which I gave him, threw one of my red blankets over his shoulders, inverted my sitz-bath on his head, helmet fashion, and made himself picturesque and comfortable. Then he crossed his ankles, while I renewed the fire, and exposed the flat, honey-combed bottoms of his prodigious feet to the grateful warmth.

"What is the matter with the bottom of your feet and the back of your legs, that they are gouged up so?"

"Infernal chillblains—I caught them clear up to the back of my head, roosting out there under Newell's farm. But I love the place; I love it as one loves his old home. There is no peace for me like

139

the peace I feel when I am there."

We talked along for half an hour, and then I noticed that he looked tired, and spoke of it. "Tired?" he said. "Well, I should think so. And now I will tell you all about it, since you have treated me so well. I am the spirit of the Petrified Man that lies across the street there in the Museum. I am the ghost of the Cardiff Giant. I can have no rest, no peace, till they have given that poor body burial again. Now what was the most natural thing for me to do, to make men satisfy this wish? Terrify them into it!—haunt the place where the body lay! So I haunted the museum night after night. I even got other spirits to help me. But it did no good, for nobody ever came to the museum at midnight. Then it occurred to me to come over the way and haunt this place a little. I felt that if I ever got a hearing I must succeed, for I had the most efficient company that perdition could furnish. Night after night we have shivered around through these mildewed halls, dragging chains, groaning, whispering, tramping up and down stairs, till, to tell you the truth, I am almost worn out. But when I saw a light in your room tonight I roused my energies again and went at it with a deal of the old freshness. But I am tired out—entirely fagged out. Give me, I beseech you, give me some hope!"

I lit off my perch in a burst of excitement, and exclaimed:

"This transcends everything—everything that ever did occur! Why you poor blundering old fossil, you have had all your trouble for nothing—you have been haunting a PLASTER CAST of yourself—the real Cardiff Giant is in Albany!

Confound it, don't you know your own remains?"

I never saw such an eloquent look of shame, of pitiable humiliation, overspread a countenance before.

The Petrified Man rose slowly to his feet, and said:

"Honestly, IS that true?"

"As true as I am sitting here."

He took the pipe from his mouth and laid it on the mantel, then stood irresolute a moment (unconsciously, from old habit, thrusting his hands where his pantaloons pockets should have been, and meditatively dropping his chin on his breast), and finally said:

"Well—I NEVER felt so absurd before. The Petrified Man has sold everybody else, and now the mean fraud has ended by selling its own ghost! My son, if there is any charity left in your heart for a poor friendless phantom like me, don't let this get out. Think how YOU would feel if you had made such an ass of yourself."

I heard his stately tramp die away, step by step down the stairs and out into the deserted street, and felt sorry that he was gone, poor fellow—and sorrier still that he had carried off my red blanket and my bath tub.

The Day of the Dead

The Day of the Dead is a traditional Mexican holiday that commemorates and honors the death of loved family members and friends. Despite its spooky name, the Day of the Dead is a festive celebration of devotion and remembrance, that lasts for two days in early November every year.

As the holiday approaches, families prepare altars in their homes by filling them with flowers, candles, and photos of lost loved ones. Symbolic gifts, such as breads or sugar skeletons are presented by friends and neighbors and added to the shrines. On November 1st, households throughout Mexico carry the contents of their altars to their local cemeteries where they spend the night at the gravesites of their lost relatives, telling stories and talking to the spirits of the dead. In the morning, the mourners return home in high spirits to celebrate with music and lavish feasts. As dusk sets in, doors and windows are pushed open so that any remaining spirits may wander in and join the revelry.

WITCHES' BREW

This delicious fruity drink will give you a magical boost on those cold winter nights. While the cauldron can be substituted with a regular pot, you may find the brew loses some of its potency. For a little extra zip, add a few drops of full moon water just before serving.

3 cups apple cider
1 cup cranberry juice
1 stick cinnamon
1 teaspoon whole cloves
1 tablespoon honey

1. Put all ingredients in a small cauldron on the stove.
2. Heat well, but do not boil.
3. Strain out cloves and cinnamon stick.
4. Serve hot in mugs. (Goes very well with Gingerbread Ghosts!)

THE CURSE OF
THE HINEMOA

In 1892, the ship Hinemoa—named after the beautiful and graceful daughter of a very powerful New Zealand chief—set sail on a chilling journey of terror. A ghastly string of bad luck for its first captains revealed that something was terribly wrong with the steamer. The first captain went insane and had to be replaced. The next fell victim of foul play and was thrown into prison. The third man at the helm became a drunk and, shaking from DT's, lost his job. Captain number four mysteriously died in his cabin, and on the fifth voyage, the captain committed suicide.

The next time the Hinemoa went to sea, it lost its balance and overturned. Righted again, it set sail once more and put its curse on two sailors, washing them overboard into the Pacific.

The curse continued until the last voyage of the Hinemoa in September 1917, Instead of a graceful

retirement, the unfortunate vessel was unlucky enough
to cross paths with an deadly German submarine.
Shortly thereafter, the Hinemoa sank, bringing the
curse to a watery end.

The Hinemoa's faithful crew knew why the ship was
cursed. Deadly forces entered the ship while it was being
built, they claimed, and were stored up in the heart of
the vessel. How did they arrive, and in what material?
The first ballast—heavy material used to give the ship
stability—was gravel from a London graveyard.

salt

Sprinkle salt at the doorstep of a new home, so evil spirits will never enter. Do not hand a salt shaker to a guest at your table. Place it down first. Remember, "to pass salt is to pass sorrow." It is understood that when we spill salt, friendly spirits to our right are warning us that evil approaches on the left, so toss a pinch of salt its way to stave off danger.

For thousands of years, superstitions about salt have been incorporated into religious, domestic and business practices. Because salt could preserve food, people thought it had the power to protect them as well. Salt was poured into to wells to purify water against evil and was placed on the chest of a corpse before burial. Believing it lengthened life, mothers even salted their babies.

In biblical times, people ceremoniously ate salt to ensure business agreements would remain true (hence the expression "a covenant of salt.") Not always considered good luck, it was forbidden to speak the word "salt" while at sea for fear of the consequences.

Even in the supernatural world salt is relied upon. It is often placed in the corners of a room before a spell is cast and the harmful spells of others are known to be broken with a ritual salt bath.

The Vampire
by Rudyard Kipling

A fool there was and he made his prayer
  (Even as you and I!)
To a rag and a bone and a hank of hair
  (We called her the woman who
  did not care)
But the fool he called her his lady fair—
  (Even as you and I!)

Oh, the years we waste and the tears
  we waste
And the work of our head and hand
Belong to the woman who did not know
  (And now we know that she
  never could know)
And did not understand!

A fool there was and his goods he spent
  (Even as you and I!)
Honour and faith and a sure intent
  (And it wasn't the least what the lady meant)

150

But a fool must follow his natural bent
   (Even as you and I!)

Oh, the toil we lost and the spoil we lost
  And the excellent things we planned
    Belong to the woman who didn't know why
        (And now we know that she never knew why)
  And did not understand!

The fool was stripped to his foolish hide
      (Even as you and I!)
  Which she might have seen when she threw him aside—
      (But it isn't on record the lady tried)
  So some of him lived but the most of him died—
    (Even as you and I!)

And it isn't the shame and it isn't the blame
  That stings like a white-hot brand—
  It's coming to know that she never knew why
  (Seeing, at last, she could never know why)
And never could understand!

THE MONKEY'S PAW

BY W. W. JACOBS

Without, the night was cold and wet, but in the small parlor of Lakesnam Villa the blinds were drawn and the fire burned brightly. Father and son were at chess, the former, who possessed ideas about the game involving radical changes, putting his king into such sharp and unnecessary perils that it even provoked comment from the white-haired old lady knitting placidly by the fire.

"Hark at the wind," said Mr. White, who, having seen a fatal mistake after it was too late, was amiably desirous of preventing his son from seeing it.

"I'm listening," said the latter, grimly surveying the board as he stretched out his hand. "Check."

"I should hardly think that he'd come tonight," said his father, with his hand poised over the board.

"Mate," replied the son.

"That's the worst of living so far out," bawled Mr. White, with sudden and unlooked-for violence; "of all the beastly, slushy, out-of-the-way places to live in, this is the worst. Pathway's a bog, and the road's a torrent. I don't know what people are thinking about. I suppose because only two houses on the road are let, they think it doesn't matter."

"Never mind, dear," said his wife soothingly; "perhaps you'll win the next one."

Mr. White looked up sharply, just in time to intercept a knowing glance between mother and son. The words died away on his lips, and he hid a guilty grin in his thin gray beard.

"There he is," said Herbert White, as the gate banged to loudly and heavy footsteps came toward the door.

The old man rose with hospitable haste, and opening the door, was heard condoling with the new arrival. The new arrival also condoled with himself, so that Mrs. White said, "Tut, tut!" and coughed gently as her husband entered the room, followed by a tall burly man, beady of eye and rubicund of visage.

"Sergeant Major Morris," he said, introducing him.

The sergeant major shook hands, and taking the proffered seat by the fire, watched contentedly while his host got out whisky and tumblers and stood a small copper kettle on the fire.

At the third glass his eyes got brighter, and he began to talk, the little family circle regarding with eager interest this visitor from distant parts, as he squared his broad shoulders in the chair and spoke of strange scenes and doughty deeds, of wars and plagues and strange peoples.

"Twenty-one years of it," said Mr. White, nodding at his wife and son. "When he went away he was a slip of a youth in the warehouse. Now look at him."

"He don't look to have taken much harm," said Mrs. White politely.

"I'd like to go to India myself," said the old man, "just to look round a bit, you know."

"Better where you are," said the sergeant major, shaking his head. He put down the empty glass and, sighing softly, shook it again.

"I should like to see those old temples and fakirs and jugglers," said the old man. "What was that you started telling me the other day about a monkey's paw or something, Morris?"

"Nothing," said the soldier hastily. "Leastways, nothing worth hearing."

"Monkey's paw?" said Mrs. White curiously.

"Well, it's just a bit of what you might call magic, perhaps," said the sergeant major offhandedly.

His three listeners leaned forward eagerly. The visitor absent-mindedly put his empty glass to his lips and then set it down again. His host filled it for him.

"To look at," said the sergeant major, fumbling in his pocket, "it's just an ordinary little paw, dried to a mummy."

He took something out of his pocket and proffered it. Mrs. White drew back with a grimace, but her son, taking it, examined it curiously.

"And what is there special about it?" inquired Mr. White, as he took it from his son and, having examined it, placed it upon the table.

"It had a spell put on it by an old fakir," said the sergeant major, "a very holy man. He wanted to show that fate ruled people's lives, and that those who interfered with it did so to their sorrow. He put a spell on it so that three separate men could have three wishes from it."

His manner was so impressive that his hearers were conscious that their light laughter jarred somewhat.

"Well, why don't you have three, sir?" said Herbert White cleverly.

The soldier regarded him in the way that middle age is wont to regard presumptuous youth. "I have," he said quietly, and his blotchy face whitened.

"And did you really have the three wishes granted?" asked Mrs. White.

"I did," said the sergeant major, and his glass tapped against his strong teeth.

"And has anybody else wished?" inquired the old lady.

"The first man had his three wishes, yes," was the reply. "I don't know what the first two were, but the third was for death. That's how I got the paw."

His tones were so grave that a hush fell upon the group.

"If you've had your three wishes, it's no good to you now, then, Moris," said the old man at last. "What do you keep it for?"

The soldier shook his head. "Fancy, I suppose," he said slowly. "I did have some idea of selling it, but I don't think I will. It has caused enough mischief already. Besides, people won't buy. They think it's a fairy tale, some of them, and those who do think anything of it want to try it first and pay me afterward."

"If you could have another three wishes," said the old man, eyeing him keenly, "would you have them?"

"I don't know," said the other. "I don't know."

He took the paw, and dangling it between his front finger and thumb, suddenly threw it upon the fire. White, with a slight cry, stooped down and snatched it off.

"Better let it burn," said the soldier solemnly.

"If you don't want it, Morris," said the old man, "give it to me."

"I won't," said his friend doggedly. "I threw it on the fire. If you keep it, don't blame me for what happens. Pitch it on the fire again, like a sensible man."

The other shook his head and examined his new possession closely. "How do you do it?" he inquired.

"Hold it up in your right hand and wish aloud," said the sergeant major, "but I warn you of the consequences."

"Sounds like the *Arabian Nights*," said Mrs. White, as she rose and began to set the supper. "Don't you think you might wish for four pairs of hands for me?"

Her husband drew the talisman from his pocket and then all three burst into laughter as the sergeant major, with a look of alarm on his face, caught him by the arm.

"If you must wish," he said gruffly, "wish for something sensible."

Mr. White dropped it back into his pocket, and placing chairs, motioned his friend to the table. In the business of supper the talisman was partly forgotten, and afterward the three sat listening in an enthralled fashion to a second installment of the soldier's adventures in India.

"If the tale about the monkey's paw is not more truthful than those he has been telling us," said Herbert, as the door closed behind their guest, just in time for him to catch the last train, "we shan't make much out of it."

"Did you give him anything for it, father?" inquired Mrs. White, regarding her husband closely.

"A trifle," said he, coloring slightly. "He didn't want it, but I made him take it. And he pressed me again to throw it away."

"Likely," said Herbert, with pretended horror. "Why, we're going to be rich, and famous, and happy. Wish to be an emperor, father, to begin with; then you can't be henpecked."

He darted round the table, pursued by the maligned Mrs. White armed with an antimacassar.

Mr. White took the paw from his pocket and eyed it dubiously. "I don't know what to wish for, and that's a fact," he said slowly. "It seems to me I've got all I want."

"If you only cleared the house, you'd be quite happy, wouldn't you?" said Herbert, with his hand on his shoulder. "Well, wish for two hundred pounds, then; that'll just do it."

His father, smiling shamefacedly at his own credulity, held up the talisman, as his son, with a solemn face somewhat marred by a wink at his mother, sat down at the piano and struck a few impressive chords.

"I wish for two hundred pounds," said the old man distinctly.

A fine crash from the piano greeted the words, interrupted by a shuddering cry from the old man. His wife and son ran toward him.

"It moved," he cried, with a glance of disgust at the object as it lay on the floor. "As I wished it twisted in my hands like a snake."

"Well, I don't see the money," said his son, as he picked it up and placed it on the table, "and I bet I never shall."

"It must have been your fancy, father," said his wife, regarding him anxiously.

He shook his head. "Never mind, though; there's no harm done, but it gave me a shock all the same."

They sat down by the fire again while the two men finished their pipes. Outside, the wind was higher than ever, and the old man started nervously at the sound of a door banging upstairs. A silence unusual and depressing settled upon all three, which lasted until the old couple rose to retire for the night.

"I expect you'll find the cash tied up in a big bag in the middle of your bed," said Herbert, as he bade them good night, "and something horrible squatting up on top of the wardrobe watching you as you pocket your ill-gotten gains."

II.

In the brightness of the wintry sun next morning as it streamed over the breakfast table, Herbert laughed at his fears. There was an air of prosaic wholesomeness about the room which it had lacked on the previous night, and the dirty, shriveled little paw was pitched on the sideboard with a carelessness which betokened no great belief in its virtues.

"I suppose all old soldiers are the same," said Mrs. White. "The idea of our listening to such nonsense! How could wishes be granted in these days? And if they could, how could two hundred pounds hurt you, father?"

"Might drop on his head from the sky," said the frivolous Herbert.

"Morris said the things happened so naturally," said his father, "that you might if you so wished attribute it to coincidence."

"Well, don't break into the money before I come back," said Herbert, as he rose from the table. "I'm afraid it'll turn you into a mean, avaricious man, and we shall have to disown you."

His mother laughed, and following him to the door, watched him down the road, and returning to the breakfast table, was very happy at the expense of her husband's credulity. All of which did not prevent her from scurrying to the door at the postman's knock, nor prevent her from referring somewhat shortly to retired sergeant majors of bibulous habits when she found that the post brought a tailor's bill.

"Herbert will have some more of his funny remarks, I expect, when he comes home," she said, as they sat at dinner.

"I dare say," said Mr. White, pouring himself out some beer; "but for all that, the thing moved in my hand; that I'll swear to."

"You thought it did," said the old lady soothingly.

"I say it did," replied the other. "There was no thought about it; I had just—What's the matter?"

His wife made no reply. She was watching the mysterious movements of a man outside, who, peering in an undecided fashion at the house, appeared to be trying to make up his mind to enter. In mental connection with the two hundred pounds, she noticed that the stranger was well-dressed and wore a silk hat of glossy newness. Three times he paused at the gate, and then walked on again. The fourth time he stood with his hand upon it, and then with sudden resolution flung it open and walked up the path. Mrs. White at the same moment placed her hands behind her, and hurriedly unfastening the strings of her apron, put that useful article of apparel beneath the cushion of her chair.

She brought the stranger, who seemed ill at ease, into the room. He gazed furtively at Mrs. White, and listened in a preoccupied fashion as the old lady apologized for the appearance of the room, and her husband's coat, a garment which he usually reserved for the garden. She then waited as patiently as her sex would permit for him to broach his business, but he was at first strangely silent.

"I—was asked to call," he said at last, and stooped and picked a piece of cotton from his trousers. "I come from Maw and Meggins."

The old lady started. "Is anything the matter?" she asked breathlessly. "Has anything happened to Herbert? What is it? What is it?"

Her husband interposed. "There, there, mother," he said hastily. "Sit down, and don't jump to conclusions. You've not brought bad news, I'm sure, sir," and he eyed the other wistfully.

"I'm sorry—" began the visitor.

"Is he hurt?" demanded the mother.

The visitor bowed in assent. "Badly hurt," he said quietly, "but he is not in any pain."

"Oh, thank God!" said the old woman, clasping her hands. "Thank God for that! Thank—"

She broke off suddenly as the sinister meaning of the assurance dawned upon her and she saw the awful confirmation of her fears in the other's averted face. She caught her breath, and turning to her slower-witted husband, laid her trembling old hand upon his. There was a long silence.

"He was caught in the machinery," said the visitor at length, in a low voice.

"Caught in the machinery," repeated Mr. White, in a dazed fashion, "yes."

163

He sat staring blankly out at the window, and taking his wife's hand between his own, pressed it as he had been wont to do in their old courting days nearly forty years before.

"He was the only one left us," he said, turning gently to the visitor. "It is hard."

The other coughed, and rising, walked slowly to the window. "The firm wished me to convey their sincere sympathy with you in your great loss," he said, without looking round. "I beg that you will understand I am only their servant and merely obeying orders."

There was no reply; the old woman's face was white, her eyes staring, and her breath inaudible; on the husband's face was a look such as his friend the sergeant might have carried into his first action.

"I was to say that Maw and Meggins disclaim all responsibility," continued the other. "They admit no liability at all, but in consideration of your son's services they wish to present you with a certain sum as compensation."

Mr. White dropped his wife's hand, and rising to his feet, gazed with a look of horror at his visitor. His dry lips shaped the words, "How much?"

"Two hundred pounds," was the answer.

Unconscious of his wife's shriek, the old man smiled faintly, put out his hands like a sightless man, and dropped, a senseless heap, to the floor.

III.

In the huge new cemetery, some two miles distant, the old people buried their dead, and came back to a house steeped in shadow and silence. It was all over so quickly that at first they could hardly realize it, and remained in a state of expectation as though of something else to happen—something else which was to lighten this load, too heavy for old hearts to bear. But the days passed, and expectation gave place to resignation—the hopeless resignation of the old, sometimes miscalled apathy. Sometimes they hardly exchanged a word, for now they had nothing to talk about, and their days were long to weariness.

It was about a week after that that the old man, waking suddenly in the night, stretched out his hand and found himself alone. The room was in darkness, and the sound of subdued weeping came from the window. He raised himself in bed and listened.

"Come back," he said tenderly. "You will be cold."

"It is colder for my son," said the old woman, and wept afresh.

The sound of her sobs died away on his ears. The bed was warm, and his eyes heavy with sleep. He dozed fitfully, and then slept until a sudden wild cry from his wife awoke him with a start.

"The monkey's paw!" she cried wildly. "The monkey's paw!"

He started up in alarm. "Where? Where is it? What's the matter?"

She came stumbling across the room toward him. "I want it," she said quietly. "You've not destroyed it?"

"It's in the parlor, on the bracket," he replied, marveling. "Why?"

She cried and laughed together, and bending over, kissed his cheek.

"I only just thought of it," she said hysterically. "Why didn't I think of it before? Why didn't you think of it?"

"Think of what?" he questioned.

"The other two wishes," she replied rapidly. "We've only had one."

"Was not that enough?" he demanded fiercely.

"No," she cried triumphantly; "we'll have one more. Go down and get it quickly, and wish our boy alive again."

The man sat up in bed and flung the bedclothes from his quaking limbs. "Good God, you are mad!" he cried, aghast.

"Get it," she panted; "get it quickly, and wish—Oh, my boy, my boy!"

Her husband struck a match and lit the candle. "Get back to bed," he said unsteadily. "You don't know what you are saying."

"We had the first wish granted," said the old woman feverishly; "why not the second?"

"A coincidence," stammered the old man.

"Go and get it and wish," cried the old woman, and dragged him toward the door.

He went down in the darkness, and felt his way to the parlor, and then to the mantelpiece. The talisman was in its place, and a horrible fear that the unspoken wish might bring his mutilated son before him ere he could escape from the room seized upon him, and he caught his breath as he found that he had lost the direction of the door. His brow cold with sweat, he felt his way round the table, and groped along the wall until he found himself in the small passage with the unwholesome thing in his hand.

Even his wife's face seemed changed as he entered the room. It was white and expectant, and to his fears seemed to have an unusual look upon it. He was afraid of her.

"Wish!" she cried, in a strong voice.

"It is foolish and wicked," he faltered.

"Wish!" repeated his wife.

He raised his hand. "I wish my son alive again."

The talisman fell to the floor, and he regarded it shudderingly. Then he sank trembling into a chair as the old woman, with burning eyes, walked to the window and raised the blind.

He sat until he was chilled with the cold, glancing occasionally at the figure of the old woman peering through the window. The candle end, which had burnt below the rim of the china candlestick, was throwing pulsating shadows on the ceiling and walls, until, with a flicker larger than the rest, it expired. The old man, with an unspeakable sense of relief at the failure of the talisman, crept back to his bed, and a minute or two afterward the old woman came silently and apathetically beside him.

Neither spoke, but both lay silently listening to the ticking of the clock. A stair creaked, and a squeaky mouse scurried noisily through the wall. The darkness was oppressive, and after lying for some time screwing up his courage, the husband took the box of matches, and striking one, went downstairs for a candle.

At the foot of the stairs the match went out, and he paused to strike another, and at the same moment a knock, so quiet and stealthy as to be scarcely audible, sounded on the front door.

The matches fell from his hand. He stood motionless, his breath suspended until the knock was repeated. Then he turned and fled swiftly back to his room, and closed the door behind him. A third knock sounded through the house.

"What's that?" cried the old woman, starting up.

"A rat," said the old man, in shaking tones— "a rat. it passed me on the stairs."

His wife sat up in bed, listening. A loud knock resounded through the house.

"It's Herbert!" she screamed. "It's Herbert!"

She ran to the door, but her husband was before her, and catching her by the arm, held her tightly.

"What are you going to do?" he whispered hoarsely.

"It's my boy; it's Herbert!" she cried, struggling mechanically. "I forgot it was two miles away. What are you holding me for? Let go. I must open the door."

"For God's sake don't let it in," cried the old man, trembling.

"You're afraid of your own son," she cried, struggling. "Let me go. I'm coming, Herbert; I'm coming."

There was another knock, and another. The old woman with a sudden wrench broke free and ran from the room. Her husband followed to the landing, and called after her appealingly as she hurried downstairs. He heard the chain rattle back and the bottom bolt drawn slowly and stiffly from the socket. Then the old woman's voice, strained and panting.

"The bolt," she cried loudly. "Come down. I can't reach it."

But her husband was on his hands and knees groping wildly on the floor in search of the paw. If he could only find it before the thing outside got in. A perfect fusillade of knocks reverberated through the house, and he heard the scraping of a chair as his wife put it down in the passage against the door. He heard the creaking of the bolt as it came slowly back, and at the same moment, he found the monkey's paw, and frantically breathed his third and last wish.

The knocking ceased suddenly, although the echoes of it were still in the house. He heard the chair drawn back and the door opened. A cold wind rushed up the staircase, and a long loud wail of disappointment and misery from his wife gave him courage to run down to her side, and then to the gate beyond. The street lamp flickering opposite shone on a quiet and deserted road.

The Raven
by Edgar Allan Poe

Once upon a midnight dreary, while I pondered, weak and weary,
Over many a quaint and curious volume of forgotten lore—
While I nodded, nearly napping, suddenly there came a tapping,
As of some one gently rapping, rapping at my chamber door.
"'Tis some visitor," I muttered, tapping at my chamber door—
     Only this and nothing more."

Ah, distinctly I remember it was in the bleak December,
And each separate dying ember wrought its ghost upon the floor.
Eagerly I wished the morrow;—vainly I had sought to borrow
From my books surcease of sorrow—sorrow for the lost Lenore—
For the rare and radiant maiden whom the angels name Lenore—
     Nameless here for evermore.

Open here I flung the shutter, when, with many a flirt and flutter,
In there stepped a stately Raven of the saintly days of yore.
Not the least obeisance made he; not a minute stopped or stayed he,
But, with mien of lord or lady, perched above my chamber door—
Perched upon a bust of Pallas just above my chamber door—
     Perched, and sat, and nothing more.

Then this ebony bird beguiling my sad fancy into smiling,
By the grave and stern decorum of the countenance it wore,
"Though thy crest be shorn and shaven, thou," I said, "art sure no craven,
Ghastly grim and ancient Raven wandering from the Nightly shore—
Tell me what thy lordly name is on the Night's Plutonian shore!"
          Quoth the Raven, "Nevermore."

Much I marvelled this ungainly fowl to hear discourse so plainly,
Though its answer little meaning—little relevancy bore;
For we cannot help agreeing that no living human being
Ever yet was blessed with seeing bird above his chamber door—
Bird or beast upon the sculptured bust above his chamber door,
          With such name as "Nevermore."

But the Raven, sitting lonely on that placid bust, spoke only
That one word, as if his soul in that one word he did outpour.
Nothing farther then he uttered; not a feather then he fluttered—
Till I scarcely more than muttered: "Other friends have flown before—
On the morrow he will leave me as my Hopes have flown before."
          Then the bird said, "Nevermore."

Startled at the stillness broken by reply so aptly spoken,
"Doubtless," said I, "what it utters is its only stock and store,
Caught from some unhappy master whom unmerciful Disaster

Followed fast and followed faster till his songs one burden bore—
Till the dirges of his Hope that melancholy burden bore
            Of 'Never—nevermore.'"

But the Raven still beguiling all my sad soul into smiling,
Straight I wheeled a cushioned seat in front of bird and bust and door;
Then, upon the velvet sinking, I betook myself to linking
Fancy unto fancy, thinking what this ominous bird of yore—
What this grim, ungainly, ghastly, gaunt, and ominous bird of your
            Meant in croaking "Nevermore."

Be that word our sign of parting, bird or fiend!" I shrieked, upstarting—
"Get thee back into the tempest and the Night's Plutonian shore!
Leave no black plume as a token of that lie thy soul hath spoken!
Leave my loneliness unbroken!—quit the bust above my door!
Take thy beak from out my heart, and take thy form from off my door!"
            Quoth the Raven, "Nevermore."

And the Raven, never flitting, still is sitting, still is sitting
On the pallid bust of Pallas just above my chamber door;
And his eyes have all the seeming of a demon's that is dreaming,
And the lamp-light o'er him streaming throws his shadow on the floor;
And my soul from out that shadow that lies floating on the floor
            Shall be lifted—nevermore!

THE BLACK CAT

The black cat is the most commonly thought enchanted animal of the mystical world. Everyone knows that when a black cat crosses your path, bad luck is soon to follow. But did you know that you could counteract this evil omen with a few simple tricks? As soon as you spot the feline, spit on the ground, turn yourself around three times, or walk backward retracing your steps. For extra insurance, try reciting the following incantation:

> *Black Cat, I do pray,*
> *Bring me luck and bless my way*
> *Do not choose to bring me harm*
> *Let me pass with this small charm*

As you pass, reach down and stroke the cat's back, as a gesture of kindness.

Often the companions of witches, black cats are believed to have the power to reason, perform sorcery, and understand human languages. Many members of the magical order believe the Devil takes the form of the shadowy feline when he goes about his dark business. So the next time a black cat crosses your path, beware! It just may be the Devil in disguise . . .

Revenge an Enemy Spell

This spell is not to be taken lightly and should only be used when all other non-magical remedies have failed. If you wish to stop the antics or trickery of an enemy and get revenge, this time-honored charm will work without fail. Simply write the name of your rival on a small piece of paper, roll it into a tiny ball, and place it in an empty mug along with a strand of the person's hair. Fill the mug with water and, as you hide it away in the depths of your freezer, recite aloud, "May your teeth chatter and your stomach grow fatter!" The moment the water hardens into ice, the spell will take effect. But be warned! If the ice should melt, the spell will be instantly broken. So defrost at your own risk!

ARE YOU DEAD OR ALIVE?

Command your heartbeat to stop and start again with this easy yet amazing trick.

Bunch up a hand towel into a hard ball and secretly place it under your arm.

Insert a thumbtack into the end of a wooden match stick. Place this on your wrist over your pulse.

Ask your audience to step up and take a close look at the moving match stick. With each heartbeat, the match shakes.

Point at the match and say, "Abracadabra—STOP!" At the same time, tightly squeeze the towel under your arm.

The pressure has slowed down the blood flow to your wrist, and the match no longer moves. Invite your audience to look closely, saying, "My heart has stopped at my command."

Then say, "I command you to COME TO LIFE!" Relax your arm and let the blood flow strongly again. The match will immediately start to move with your pulse.

THE CURSE OF
THE SCREAMING SKULL

Found in the town of Bettiscombe, snuggled in the heart of the English countryside, is the famous and terrifying legend of the screaming skull.

The story goes that during the 17th century a resident of Bettiscombe, Azariah Pinney, returned home after living abroad in the West Indies for some years. Azariah brought with him a slave to help care for his house and property, known as Bettiscombe Manor. The slave, however, soon fell ill and, lying upon his deathbed, made a last desperate request to his master. He asked that his corpse be sent home and buried in the land of his birth. Azariah agreed. But as soon as the slave had passed, Azariah broke his promise and buried the slave in a nearby churchyard cemetery.

The gravedigger had no sooner shoveled the last pile of dirt onto the casket, when a strange moaning drifted up through the fresh earth. Before long, the moaning turned into an endless agonizing scream, which tore through the quiet country-side like a nightmare. The local villagers demanded that Azariah dig up the body and remove it from the cemetery immediately. So the slave was returned to Bettiscombe Manor, where Azariah stored the body in the attic. There the tortured screams ceased. The corpse remained in Azariah's home, where it decayed over time, until all that remained was the skull.

As the years passed, Bettiscombe Manor saw many owners come and go. Some did not take well to sleeping so near the infamous screaming skull and made the mistake of removing it from its resting place. One owner threw the skull into a nearby pond one stormy summer night, thinking it would sink to a watery grave. But the skull rose to the surface shrieking in anguish. Another family buried the offensive fossil in the backyard garden, but it quickly dug itself out of the ground. Ultimately, the skull was returned to the house, where it resides peacefully to this day.

ROASTED PUMPKIN SEEDS

Instead of throwing away those slippery pumpkin seeds when
you carve your jack-o-lantern, put them aside and roast them
later for a tasty Halloween treat.

1 ½ cups pumpkin seeds
2 tablespoons of butter
Salt to taste

1. Preheat oven to 300°F.
2. Scoop out seeds from a fresh
   pumpkin. Wash seeds under cold
   water, removing any stringy fibers.
   Blot dry with paper towels and set
   aside in a bowl.

3. Melt butter in a saucepan and pour
   over the bowl of seeds. Sprinkle
   with salt to taste and mix until the
   seeds are well coated.

4. Spread the pumpkin seeds evenly
   in a single layer on a baking sheet.
   Bake for approximately 45 minutes,
   stirring occasionally, until seeds
   are golden brown.

The Story of the Jack-o'-Lantern

A long time ago an Irishman named Jack found himself face to face with the Devil while sipping whiskey at a local pub. Satan had come to claim Jack's soul. But Jack, a con artist to the core, tricked the Devil into climbing a nearby tree on a dare. No sooner had the Dark Prince triumphantly reached the top branch, when Jack quickly pulled out a knife and carved a crucifix into the trunk, trapping the Devil in the tree.

Jack escaped that night with his soul intact, but continued to live out the rest of his days as a trickster and a drunk. When he died at a ripe old age, Jack was turned away from Heaven's gates for living such a dishonest and sinful life. So arriving at Hell's flaming threshold, Jack found himself staring into Satan's eyes once again. The devil fixed him with an evil glare and

184

refused him entry into the fiery pit. Stranded in the blackness between Heaven and Hell, Jack begged the Devil for a candle to light his way. The Devil threw him a burning coal and turned his back on Jack forever. Jack placed the ember in a carved out turnip, using it as a lantern as he wandered the netherworlds in anguish.

The Jack-o'-Lantern soon became the Irish symbol for a damned soul and was often placed in a window on Halloween to scare off evil spirits. When the Irish later immigrated to America, they began using pumpkins to make these superstitious lanterns instead of turnips, which were less plentiful and harder to come by. Today, Jack-o'-Lanterns are a favorite Halloween tradition, used as spooky decorations rather than spiritual watchmen.

THE LEGEND OF SLEEPY HOLLOW

BY WASHINGTON IRVING

In the bosom of one of those spacious coves which indent the eastern shore of the Hudson, at that broad expansion of the river denominated by the ancient Dutch navigators the Tappan Zee, and where they always prudently shortened sail, and implored the protection of St. Nicholas when they crossed, there lies a small market town or rural port, which by some is called Greensburgh, but which is more generally and properly known by the name of Tarry Town. Not far from this village, perhaps about two miles, there is a little valley, or rather lap of land, among high hills, which is one of the quietest places in the whole world. A small brook glides through it, with just murmur enough to lull one to repose; and the occasional whistle of a quail, or tapping of a woodpecker, is almost the only sound that ever breaks in upon the uniform tranquility.

From the listless repose of the place, and the peculiar character of its inhabitants, who are descendants from the original Dutch settlers, this sequestered glen has long been known by the name of Sleepy

Hollow, and its rustic lads are called the Sleepy Hollow Boys throughout all the neighboring country. A drowsy, dreamy influence seems to hang over the land, and to pervade the very atmosphere. Some say that the place was bewitched by a high German doctor, during the early days of the settlement; others, that an old Indian chief, the prophet or wizard of his tribe, held his pow-wows there before the country was discovered by Master Hendrick Hudson. Certain it is, the place still continues under the sway of some bewitching power, that holds a spell over the minds of the good people, causing them to walk in a continual reverie. They are given to all kinds of marvellous beliefs; are subject to trances and visions; and frequently see strange sights, and hear music and voices in the air. The whole neighborhood abounds with local tales, haunted spots, and twilight superstitions; stars shoot and meteors glare oftener across the valley than in any other part of the country, and the nightmare, with her whole ninefold, seems to make it the favorite scene of her gambols.

The dominant spirit, however, that haunts this enchanted region, and seems to be commander-in-chief of all the powers of the air, is the apparition of a figure on horseback without a head. It is said by some to be the ghost of a Hessian trooper, whose head had been carried away by a cannon-ball, in some nameless battle during the Revolutionary War, and who is ever and anon seen by the country folk, hurrying along in the gloom of night, as if on the wings of the wind. His haunts are not confined to the valley, but extend at times to the adjacent roads, and especially to the vicinity of a church at no great distance. Indeed, certain of the most authentic historians of those parts, who have been careful in collecting and collating the floating facts concerning this spectre, allege that the body of the trooper, having been buried in the church-yard, the ghost rides forth to the scene of battle in nightly quest of his head; and that the rushing speed with which he sometimes passes along the Hollow, like a midnight blast, is owing to his being belated, and in a hurry to get back to the churchyard before daybreak.

Such is the general purport of this legendary superstition, which has furnished materials for many a wild story in that region of shadows; and the spectre is known, at all the country firesides, by the name of the Headless Horseman of Sleepy Hollow.

In this by-place of nature, there abode, in a remote period of American history, that is to say, some thirty years since, a worthy wight of the name of Ichabod Crane; who sojourned, or, as he expressed it, "tarried," in Sleepy Hollow, for the purpose of instructing the children of the vicinity.

His school-house was a low building of one large room, rudely constructed of logs; the windows partly glazed, and partly patched with leaves of old copy-books. It was most ingeniously secured at vacant hours by a whithe twisted in the handle of the door, and stakes set against the window-shutters; so that, though a thief might get in with perfect ease, he would find some embarrassment in getting out: an idea

most probably borrowed by the architect, Yost Van Houten, from the mystery of an eel-pot. The school-house stood in a rather lonely but pleasant situation, just at the foot of a woody hill, with a brook running close by, and a formidable birch-tree growing at one end of it.

The schoolmaster is generally a man of some importance in the female circle of a rural neighborhood; being considered a kind of idle, gentleman-like personage, of vastly superior taste and accomplishments to the rough country swains, and, indeed, inferior in learning only to the parson. His appearance, therefore, is apt to occasion some little stir at the tea-table of a farm-house, and the addition of a supernumerary dish of cakes or sweet-meats, or, peradventure, the parade of a silver tea-pot. Our man of letters, therefore, was peculiarly happy in the smiles of all the country damsels. How he would figure among them in the church-yard, between services on Sundays! gathering grapes for them from the wild vines that overrun the surrounding trees; reciting for their amuse-ment all the epitaphs on the tombstones; or sauntering, with a whole bevy of them, along the banks of the adjacent mill-pond; while the more bashful country bumpkins hung sheepishly back, envying his superior elegance and address.

Another of his sources of fearful pleasure was, to pass long win-ter evenings with the old Dutch wives, as they sat spinning by the fire, with a row of apples roasting and spluttering along the hearth, and listen to their marvellous tales of ghosts and goblins, and haunted fields, and haunted brooks, and haunted bridges, and haunted houses, and particularly of the headless horseman, or Galloping Hessian of the Hollow, as they sometimes called him. He would delight them equally by his anecdotes of witchcraft, and the direful omens and portentous sights and sounds in the air, which prevailed in the earlier times of Connecticut; and would frighten them woefully with speculations upon comets and shooting stars, and with the alarming fact that the world did absolutely turn round, and that they were half the time topsy-turvy!

Among the musical disciples who assembled, one evening in each week, to receive his instructions in psalmody, was Katrina Van Tassel, the daughter and only child of a substantial Dutch farmer. She was a blooming lass of fresh eighteen; plump as a partridge; ripe and melting and rosy-cheeked as one of her father's peaches, and universally famed, not merely for her beauty, but her vast expectations.

Ichabod Crane had a soft and foolish heart towards the sex; and it is not to be wondered at that so tempting a morsel soon found favor in his eyes; more especially after he had visited her in her paternal mansion. Old Baltus Van Tassel was a perfect picture of a thriving, contented, liberal-hearted farmer. He seldom, it is true, sent either his eyes or his thoughts beyond the boundaries of his own farm; but within those everything was snug, happy, and well-conditioned. He was satisfied with his wealth, but not proud of it; and piqued himself upon the hearty abundance rather than the style in which he lived. His stronghold was situated on the banks of the Hudson, in one of those green, sheltered, fertile nooks in which the Dutch farmers are so fond of nestling. A great elm-tree spread its broad branches over it; at the foot of which bubbled up a spring of the softest and sweetest water, in a little well, formed of a barrel; and then stole sparkling away through the grass, to a neighboring brook, that bubbled along among alders and dwarf willows.

From the moment Ichabod laid his eyes upon these regions of delight, the peace of his mind was at an end, and his only study was how to gain the affections of the peerless daughter of Van Tassel. In this enterprise, however, he had more real difficulties than generally fell to the lot of a knight-errant of yore, who seldom had anything but giants, enchanters, fiery dragons, and such like easily conquered adversaries, to contend with; and had to make his way merely through gates of iron and brass, and walls of adamant, to the castle-keep, where the lady of his heart was confined; all which he achieved as easily as a man would carve his way to the centre of a Christmas pie; and then the lady gave him her hand as a matter of course. Ichabod, on the contrary, had to win his way to the heart of a country coquette, beset with a labyrinth of whims and caprices, which were forever presenting new difficulties and impediments; and he had to encounter a host of fearful adversaries of real flesh and blood, the numerous rustic admirers, who beset every portal to her heart; keeping a watchful and angry eye upon each other, but ready to fly out in the common cause against any new competitor.

Among these the most formidable was a burly, roaring, roistering blade, of the name of Abraham, or, according to the Dutch abbreviation, Brom Van Brunt, the hero of the country round, which rang with his feats of strength and hardihood. He was broad shouldered and double-jointed, with short, curly black hair, and a bluff but not unpleasant countenance, having a mingled air of fun and arrogance. From his Herculean frame and great powers of limb, he had received the nickname of Brom Bones, by which he was universally known.

Brom, who had a degree of rough chivalry in his nature, would fain have carried matters to open warfare, and have settled their pretensions to the lady according to the mode of those most concise and simple reasoners, the knights-errant of yore—by single combat; but Ichabod was too conscious of the superior might of his adversary to enter the lists against him: he had overheard a boast of Bones, that he would "double the schoolmaster up, and lay him on a shelf of his own school-house;" and he was too wary to give him an opportunity. There was something extremely provoking in this obstinately pacific system; it left Brom no alternative but to draw upon the funds of rustic waggery in his disposi-

tion, and to play off boorish practical jokes upon his rival. Ichabod became the object of whimsical persecution to Bones and his gang of rough riders. They harried his hitherto peaceful domains; smoked out his singing-school, by stopping up the chimney; broke into the schoolhouse at night, in spite of its formidable fastenings of withe and window-stakes, and turned everything topsy-turvy: so that the poor schoolmaster began to think all the witches in the country held their meetings there. But what was still more annoying, Brom took opportunities of turning him into ridicule in presence of his mistress, and had a scoundrel dog whom he taught to whine in the most ludicrous manner, and introduced as a rival of Ichabod's to instruct her in psalmody.

In this way matters went on for some time, without producing any material effect on the relative situation of the contending powers. On a fine autumnal afternoon, Ichabod, in pensive mood, sat enthroned on the lofty stool whence he usually watched all the concerns of his little literary realm. In his hand he swayed a ferule, that sceptre of despotic power; the birch of justice reposed on three nails, behind the throne, a constant terror to evil-doers; while on the desk before him might be seen sundry contraband articles and prohibited weapons, detected upon the persons of idle urchins; such as half-munched apples, pop-guns, whirligigs, fly-cages, and whole legions of rampant little paper game-cocks. Apparently there had been some appalling act of justice recently inflicted, for his scholars were all busily intent upon their books, or slyly whispering behind them with one eye kept upon the master; and a kind of buzzing stillness reigned throughout the school-room. It was suddenly interrupted by the appearance of a negro, in tow-cloth jacket and trousers, a round-crowned fragment of a hat, like the cap of Mercury, and mounted on the back of a ragged, wild, half-broken colt, which he managed with a rope by way of halter. He came clattering up to the school-door with an invitation to Ichabod to attend a merry-making or "quilting frolic," to be held that evening at Mynheer Van Tassel's; and having delivered his message with that air of importance, and effort at fine language, which a negro is apt to display on petty embassies of the kind, he dashed over the brook, and was seen scampering away up the Hollow, full of the importance and hurry of his mission.

All was now bustle and hubbub in the late quiet school-room. The scholars were hurried through their lessons, without stopping at trifles; those who were nimble skipped over half with impunity, and those who were tardy had a smart application now and then in the rear, to quicken their speed, or help them over a tall word. Books were flung aside without being put away on the shelves, inkstands were overturned, benches thrown down, and the whole school was turned loose an hour before the usual time, bursting forth like a legion of young imps, yelping and racketing about the green, in joy at their early emancipation.

The gallant Ichabod now spent at least an extra half-hour at his toilet, brushing and furbishing up his best and indeed only suit of rusty black, and arranging his locks by a bit of broken looking-glass, that hung up in the school-house. That he might make his appearance before his mistress in the true style of a cavalier, he borrowed a horse from the farmer with whom he was domiciliated, a choleric old Dutchman, of the name of Hans Van Ripper, and, thus gallantly mounted, issued forth, like a knight-errant in quest of adventures. But it is meet I should, in the true spirit of romantic story, give some account of the looks and equipments of my hero and his steed. The animal he bestrode was a broken-down plough-horse, that had outlived almost everything but his viciousness. He was gaunt and shagged, with a ewe neck and a head like a hammer; his rusty mane and tail were tangled and knotted with burrs; one eye had lost its pupil, and was glaring and spectra; but the other had the gleam of a genuine devil in it. Still he must have had fire and mettle in his day, if we may judge from the name he bore of Gunpowder.

Ichabod was a suitable figure for such a steed. He rode with short stirrups, which brought his knees nearly up to the pommel of the saddle; his sharp elbows stuck out like grasshoppers'; he carried his whip perpendicularly in his hand, like a sceptre, and, as his horse jogged on, the motion of his arms was not unlike the flapping of a pair of wings.

It was toward evening that Ichabod arrived at the castle of the Heer Van

Tassel, which he found thronged with the pride and flower of the adjacent country. Old farmers, a spare leathern-faced race, in homespun coats and breeches, blue stockings, huge shoes, and magnificent pewter buckles. Their brisk withered little dames, in close crimped caps, long-waisted shortgowns, homespun petticoats, with scissors and pincushions, and gay calico pockets hanging on the outside. Buxom lasses, almost as antiquated as their mothers, excepting where a straw hat, a fine ribbon, or perhaps a white frock, gave symptoms of city innovation. The sons, in short square skirted coats with rows of stupendous brass buttons, and their hair generally queued in the fashion of the times, especially if they could procure an eel-skin for the purpose, it being esteemed, throughout the country, as a potent nourisher and strengthener of the hair.

Brom Bones, however, was the hero of the scene, having come to the gathering on his favorite steed, Daredevil, a creature, like himself, full of mettle and mischief, and which no one but himself could manage. He was, in fact, noted for preferring vicious animals, given to all kinds of tricks, which kept the rider in constant risk of his neck, for he held a tractable well-broken horse as unworthy of a lad of spirit.

Old Baltus Van Tassel moved about among his

guests with a face dilated with content and good-humor, round and jolly as the harvest-moon. His hospitable attentions were brief, but expressive, being confined to a shake of the hand, a slap on the shoulder, a loud laugh, and a pressing invitation to "fall to, and help themselves."

And now the sound of the music from the common room, or hall, summoned to the dance. The musician was an old gray-headed negro, who had been the itinerant orchestra of the neighborhood for more than half a century. His instrument was as old and battered as himself. The greater part of the time he scraped on two or three strings, accompanying every movement of the bow with a motion of the head; bowing almost to the ground, and stamping with his foot whenever a fresh couple were to start.

When the dance was at an end, Ichabod was attracted to a knot of the sager folks, who, with old Van Tassel, sat smoking at one end of the piazza, gossiping over former times, and drawing out long stories about the war.

But all these were nothing to the tales of ghosts and apparitions that succeeded. The neighborhood is rich in legendary treasures of the kind. Local tales and superstitions thrive best in these sheltered long-settled retreats; but are trampled underfoot by the shifting throng that forms the population of most of our country places. Besides, there is no encouragement for ghosts in most of our villages, for they have scarcely had time to finish their first nap, and turn themselves in their graves before their surviving friends have travelled away from the neighborhood; so that when they turn out at night to walk their rounds, they have no acquaintance left to call upon. This is perhaps the reason why we so seldom hear of ghosts, except in our long-established Dutch communities.

The immediate cause, however, of the prevalence of supernatural stories in these parts was doubtless owing to the vicinity of Sleepy Hollow. There was a contagion in the very air that blew from the haunted region; it breathed forth an atmosphere of dreams and fancies infecting all the land. Several of the Sleepy Hollow people were present at Van Tassel's and, as usual, were doling out their wild and wonderful legends. Many dismal tales were told about funeral trains, and mourning cries and wailings heard and seen about the great tree where the unfortunate Major André was taken, and which stood in the neighborhood. Some mention was made also of the woman in white, that haunted the dark glen at Raven Rock, and was often heard to shriek on winter nights before a storm, having perished there in the snow. The chief part of the stories, however, turned upon the favorite spectre of Sleep Hollow, the headless horseman, who had been heard several times of late, patrolling the country; and, it was said, tethered his horse nightly among the graves in the churchyard.

All these tales, told in that drowsy undertone with which men talk in the dark, the countenances of the listeners only now and then receiving a casual gleam from the glare of a pipe, sank deep in the mind of Ichabod. He repaid them in kind with large extracts from his invaluable author, Cotton Mather, and added many marvellous events that had taken place in his native State of Connecticut, and fearful sights which he had seen in his nightly walks about the Sleepy Hollow.

The revel now gradually broke up. The old farmers gathered together their families in their wagons, and were heard for some time rattling along the hollow roads, and over the distant hills. Some of the damsels mounted on pillions behind their favorite swains, and their light-hearted laughter, mingling with the clatter of hoofs, echoed along the silent woodlands, sounding fainter and fainter until they gradually died away—and the late scene of noise and frolic was all silent and deserted. Ichabod only lingered behind, according to the custom of country lovers, to have a tête-à-tête with the heiress, fully convinced that he was now on the high road to success. What passed at this interview I will not pretend to say, for in fact I do not know. Something, however, I fear me, must have gone wrong, for he certainly sallied forth, after no very great interval, with an air quite desolate and chop-fallen.—Oh, these women! these women! Could that girl have been playing off any of her coquettish tricks?— Was her encouragement of the poor pedagogue all a mere sham to secure her conquest of his rival?—Heaven only knows, not I!—Let it suffice to say, Ichabod stole forth with the air of one who had been sacking a hen-roost, rather than a fair lady's heart. Without looking to the right or left to notice the scene of rural wealth on which he had so often gloated, he went straight to the stable, and with several hearty cuffs and kicks, roused his steed most uncourteously from the comfortable quarters in which he was soundly sleeping, dreaming of mountains of corn and oats, and whole valleys of timothy and clover.

It was the very witching time of night that Ichabod, heavy-hearted and crestfallen, pursued his travel homewards, along the sides of the lofty hills which rise above Tarry Town, and which he had traversed so cheerily in the afternoon. The hour was as dismal as himself. Far below him, the Tappan Zee spread its dusky and indistinct waste of waters, with here and there the tall mast of a sloop riding quietly at anchor under the land. In the dead hush of midnight he could even hear the barking of the watch-dog from the opposite shore of the Hudson; but it was so vague and faint as only to give an idea of his distance from this faithful companion of man. Now and then, too, the long-drawn crowing of a cock, accidentally awakened, would sound far, far off, from some farm-house away among the hills—but it was like a dreaming sound in his car. No signs of life occurred near him, but occasionally the melancholy chirp of a cricket, or perhaps the gutteral twang of a bull-frog, from a neighboring marsh, as if sleeping uncomfortably, and turning suddenly in his bed.

204

All the stories of ghosts and goblins that he had heard in the afternoon, now came crowding upon his recollection. The night grew darker and darker; the stars seemed to sink deeper in the sky, and driving clouds occasionally hid them from his sight. He had never felt so lonely and dismal. He was, moreover, approaching the very place where many of the scenes of the ghost-stories had been laid. In the centre of the road stood an enormous tulip-tree, which towered like a giant above all the other trees of the neighborhood, and formed a kind of landmark. Its limbs were gnarled, and fantastic, large enough to form trunks for ordinary trees, twisting down almost to the earth, and rising again into the air. It was connected with the tragical story of the unfortunate André, who had been taken prisoner hard by; and was universally known by the name of Major André's tree. The common people regarded it with a mixture of respect and superstition, partly out of sympathy for the fate of its ill-starred namesake, and partly from the tales of strange sights and doleful lamentations told concerning it.

As Ichabod approached this fearful tree, he began to whistle: he thought his whistle was answered,—it was but a blast sweeping sharply through the dry branches. As he approached a little nearer, he thought he saw something white, hanging in the midst of the tree,—he paused and ceased whistling; but on looking more narrowly, perceived that it was a place where the tree had been scathed by lightning, and the white wood laid bare. Suddenly he heard a groan,—his teeth chattered and his knees smote against the saddle: it was but the rubbing of one huge bough upon another, as they were swayed about by the breeze. He passed the tree in safety; but new perils lay before him.

About two hundred yards from the tree a small brook crossed the road, and ran into a marshy and thickly wooded glen, known by the name of Wiley's swamp. A few rough logs, laid side by side, served for a bridge over this stream. On that side of the road where the book entered the wood, a group of oaks and chestnuts, matted thick with wild grape-vines, threw a cavernous gloom over it. To pass this bridge was the severest trial. It was at this identical spot that the unfortunate André was captured, and under the covert of those chestnuts and vines were the sturdy yeomen concealed who surprised him. This has ever since been considered a haunted stream, and fearful are the feelings of the school boy who has to pass it alone after dark.

As he approached the stream, his heart began to thump; he summoned up, however, all his resolution, gave his horse half a score of kicks in the ribs, and attempted to dash briskly across the bridge; but instead of starting forward, the perverse old animal made a lateral movement, and ran broadside against the fence. Ichabod, whose fears increased with the delay, jerked the reins on the other side, and kicked lustily with the contrary foot: it was all in vain; his steed started, it is true, but it was only to plunge to the opposite side of the road into a thicket of brambles and alder bushes. The schoolmaster now bestowed both whip and heel upon the starveling ribs of old Gunpowder, who dashed forward, snuffling and snorting, but came to a stand just by the bridge, with a suddenness that had nearly sent his rider sprawling over his head. Just at this moment a plashy tramp by the side of the bridge caught the sensitive ear of Ichabod. In the dark shadow of the grove, on the margin of the brook, he beheld something huge, misshapen, black, and towering. It stirred not, but seemed gathered up in the gloom, like some gigantic monster ready to spring upon the traveller.

The hair of the affrighted pedagogue rose upon his head with terror. What was to be done? To turn and fly was now too late; and besides, what chance was there of escaping ghost or goblin, if such it was, which could ride upon the wings of the wind? Summoning up, therefore, a show of courage, he demanded in stammering accents— "Who are you?" He received no reply. He repeated his demand in a still more agitated voice. Still there was no answer. Once more he cudgelled the sides of the inflexible Gunpowder, and, shutting his eyes, broke forth with involuntary fervor into a psalm-tune. Just then the shadowy object of alarm put itself in motion, and, with a scramble and a bound, stood at once in the middle of the road. Though the night was dark and dismal, yet the form of the unknown might now in some degree be

ascertained. He appeared to be a horseman of large dimensions, and mounted on a black horse of powerful frame. He made no offer of molestation or sociability, but kept aloof on one side of the road, jogging along on the blind side of old Gunpowder, who had now got over his fright and waywardness.

Ichabod, who had no relish for this strange midnight companion, now quickened his steed, in hopes of leaving him behind. The stranger, however, quickened his horse to an equal pace. Ichabod pulled up, and fell into a walk, thinking to lag behind,—the other did the same. His heart began to sink within him; he endeavored to resume his psalm-tune, but his parched tongue clove to the roof of his mouth, and he could not utter a stave. There was something in the moody and dogged silence of this pertinacious companion, that was mysterious and appalling. It was soon fearfully accounted for. On mounting a rising ground, which brought the figure of his fellow-traveller in relief against the sky, gigantic in height, and muffled in a cloak, Ichabod was horror-struck, on perceiving that he was headless!—but his horror was still more increased, on observing that the head, which should have rested on his shoulders, was carried before him on the pommel of the saddle: his terror rose to desperation; he rained a shower of kicks and blows upon Gunpowder, hoping, by a sudden movement, to give his companion the slip,—but the spectre started full jump with him. Away then they dashed, through thick and thin; stones flying, and sparks flashing at every bound. Ichabod's flimsy garments fluttered in the air, as he stretched his long lank body away over his horse's head, in the eagerness of his flight.

They had now reached the road which turns off to Sleepy Hollow; but Gunpowder, who seemed possessed with a demon, instead of keeping up it, made an opposite turn, and plunged headlong downhill to the left. This road leads through a sandy hollow, shaded by trees for about a quarter of a mile, where it crosses the bridge famous in goblin story, and just beyond swells the green knoll on which stands the whitewashed church.

As yet the panic of the steed had given his unskillful rider an apparent advantage in the chase; but just as he had got half-way through the hollow, the girths of the saddle gave way, and he felt it slipping from under him. He seized it by the pommel, and endeavored to hold it firm, but in vain; and had just time to save himself by clasping old Gunpowder round the neck, when the saddle fell to the earth, and he heard it trampled underfoot by his pursuer. For a moment, the terror of Hans Van Ripper's wrath passed across his mind—for it was his Sunday saddle; but this was no time for petty fears; the goblin was hard on his haunches; and (unskillful rider that he was!) he had much ado to maintain his seat; sometimes slipping on one side, sometimes on another, and sometimes jolted on the high ridge of his horse's backbone, with a violence that he verily feared would cleave him asunder.

An opening in the trees now cheered him with the hopes that the church-bridge was at hand. The wavering reflection of a silver star in the bosom of the brook told him that he was not mistaken. He saw the wall of the church dimly glaring under the trees beyond. "If I can but reach that bridge," thought Ichabod, "I am safe." Just then he heard the black steed panting and blowing close behind him; he even fancied that he felt his hot breath. Another convulsive kick in the ribs, and old Gunpowder sprang upon the bridge; he thundered over the resounding planks; he gained the opposite side; and now Ichabod cast a look behind to see if his pursuer should vanish, according to rule, in a flash of fire and brimstone. Just then he saw the goblin rising in his stirrups, and in the very act of hurling his head at him. Ichabod endeavored to dodge the horrible missile, but too late. It encountered his cranium with a tremendous crash,—he was tumbled headlong into the dust, and Gunpowder, the black steed, and the goblin rider, passed by like a whirlwind.

The next morning the old horse was found without his saddle, and with the bridle under his feet, soberly cropping the grass at his master's gate. Ichabod did not make his appearance at breakfast;—dinner-hour came, but no Ichabod. The boys assembled at the school-house, and strolled idly about the banks of the brook; but no schoolmaster. Hans Van Ripper now began to feel some uneasiness about the fate of poor Ichabod, and his saddle. An inquiry was set on foot, and after diligent investigation they came upon his traces. In one part of the road leading to the church was found the saddle trampled in the dirt; the tracks of horses' hoofs deeply dented in the road, and evidently at furious speed, were traced to the bridge, beyond which, on the bank of a broad part of the brook, where the water ran deep and black, was found the hat of the unfortunate Ichabod, and close beside it a shattered pumpkin.

The brook was searched, but the body of the schoolmaster was not to be discovered.

The mysterious event caused much speculation at the church on the following Sunday. Knots of gazers and gossips were collected in the churchyard, at the bridge, and at the spot where the hat and pumpkin had been found. The stories of Brouwer, of Bones, and a whole budget of others, were called to mind; and when they had diligently considered them all, and compared them with the symptoms of the present case, they shook their heads, and came to the conclusion that Ichabod had been carried off by the Galloping Hessian. As he was a bachelor, and in nobody's debt, nobody troubled his head any more about him. The school was removed to a different quarter of the Hollow, and another pedagogue reigned in his stead.

It is true, an old farmer, who had been down to New York on a visit several years after, and from whom this account of the ghastly adventure was received, brought home the intelligence that Ichabod

Crane was still alive; that he had left the neighborhood, partly through fear of the goblin and Hans Van Ripper, and partly in mortification at having been suddenly dismissed by the heiress; that he had changed his quarters to a distant part of the country; had kept school and studied law at the same time, had been admitted to the bar, turned politician, electioneered, written for the newspapers, and finally had been made a justice of the Ten Pound Court. Brom Bones too, who shortly after his rival's disappearance conducted the blooming Katrina in triumph to the altar, was observed to look exceedingly knowing whenever the story of Ichabod was related, and always burst into a hearty laugh at the mention of the pumpkin; which led some to suspect that he knew more about the matter than he chose to tell.

The old country wives, however, who are the best judges of these matters, maintain to this day that Ichabod was spirited away by supernatural means; and it is a favorite story often told about the neighborhood round the winter evening fire. The bridge became more than ever an object of superstitious awe, and that may be the reason why the road has been altered of late years, so as to approach the church by the border of the millpond. The school-house, being deserted, soon fell to decay, and was reported to be haunted by the ghost of the unfortunate pedagogue; and the plough-boy, loitering homeward of a still summer evening, has often fancied his voice at a distance, chanting a melancholy psalm-tune, among the tranquil solitudes of Sleepy Hollow.

mIRRORS

Be careful never to break a mirror. It's a long seven years of bad luck that it will bring. Should a mirror fall and break on its own, a death in the home is soon expected. Even the house where the mirror is broken is thought to remain cursed for seven years. You also invite bad luck when you look at your reflection in a mirror by candlelight.

Long ago, people looked in amazement at their reflections in water, believing it was a glimpse at their soul. When the reflected image was altered by a wave or a ripple, it meant the soul was in danger. Over time, it came to be believed that if someone broke a mirror, it took seven years for their soul to return to them.

The seven-year sentence was assigned by the Romans, who believed it took a body seven years to repair itself or, in this case, seven years to shake the bad luck.

WIZARD'S GLASS TRICK

This dinner-table trick will show your family and friends you're a magic wizard with amazing powers of balance.

Hold up a bread plate and glass, showing your audience that there are no strings, glue or other props at work. Grasp the plate as shown in the illustration, with your thumb pointing upward.

With the back of the plate always hidden from the audience, place a glass on the top rim of the plate and support it with your thumb. Swerve the plate slightly to give the impres-sion that you're using all your super-human skills to keep the glass balanced.

Invite others at the table to try the trick—and be ready to catch the glass (if it's breakable) before it falls. When everyone begs you to show them how it's done, demand a price—like extra dessert.

EYEBALL COOKIES

½ cup shortening
¼ cup brown sugar
½ teaspoon vanilla extract
1 cup flour
¼ teaspoon salt
1 egg yolk
¼ teaspoon full moon water
(see page 10)
Nutello, peanut butter, fruit jelly,
and your choice of small round candies

1. Preheat oven to 375° & grease a cookie sheet.
2. In a cast iron cauldron or large bowl, mix shortening, brown sugar, vanilla extract, flour, and salt all together until it forms a dough.
3. In a separate bowl, beat egg white and moon water.
4. Roll dough into walnut sized balls and dip each one into egg white mixture. Place on a cookie sheet 2" apart.
5. Bake cookies for 5 minutes. Remove from oven and make thumbprint in each cookie. Bake for another 10 minutes.
6. Cool cookies on tray and fill each thumbprint with Nutello, peanut butter, or your favorite fruit jelly. Then place a chocolate chip or other candy of your choice in the center to complete the eyeball.

The Abracadaba Spell

Abracadabra! This word might be the most famous magical utterance in the world. But did you know that it was originally used in a spell against fever and illness? To perform the authentic Abracadabra spell, write the letters A-B-R-A-C-A-D-A-B-R-A on a small piece of paper as shown in following diagram:

Thread a piece of string or ribbon through the paper and hang it around the neck of the feverish patient. Just as the letters of the word ABRACADABRA disappear, so should person's illness.

Test your natural talent in the magical healing arts by trying this spell out on a brother or sister who is sick with the flu.

```
ABRACADABARA
ABRACADABR
ABRACADAB
ABRACADA
ABRACAD
ABRACA
ABRAC
ABRA
ABR
ABA
A
```

Published in 2010 by Welcome Books®
An imprint of Welcome Enterprises, Inc.
6 West 18th Street, New York, NY 10011
(212) 989-3200; Fax (212) 989-3205
www.welcomebooks.com

Designer: Timothy Shaner
Project Director: Natasha Tabori Fried
Production Editor: Alice Wong
Editorial Assistants: Lawrence Chesler, Serena Longyear

Distributed to the trade in the U.S. and Canada by Random House

Library of Congress Cataloging-in-Publication data on file.

ISBN: 978-1-59962-086-2

Printed in China
First Edition
3 5 7 9 10 8 6 4 2

acknowledgments

ILLUSTRATIONS
pg. 23: Arthur Rackham; pg.214-215, 222: John Winsch; pg.37: Harold C. Earnshaw; pg. 91: E.C. Banks; pg. 118-119: K. Lederbogen; pg. 125: Edmund Dulac; pg. 126-127, 171: Hilda Austin; pg. 135: Ellen H. Claysaddle; pg. 155: R. Drang; pg. 160: Jessie Willcox Smith; pg. 203: Bufforo

RECIPES © 2001 by Lena Tabori
ADDITIONAL ORIGINAL TEXT by Antonia Felix, Katrina Fried, Kathleen King, Chris Meason
Magic trick illustrations by Megan Halsey

Every attempt has been made to obtain permission to reproduce materials protected by copyright. Where omissions may have occurred, the publisher will be happy to acknowledge this in future printings.